The Village That Raised Us

Tours of a Happy Youth

MARIA OAKS

Copyright © 2017 Maria Oaks.

All rights reserved. No part of this book may be used or reproduced by any means, graphic, electronic, or mechanical, including photocopying, recording, taping or by any information storage retrieval system without the written permission of the author except in the case of brief quotations embodied in critical articles and reviews.

Scripture quotations marked NRSV are taken from the New Revised Standard Version of the Bible, Copyright © 1989, by the Division of Christian Education of the National Council of the Churches of Christ in the United States of America. Used by permission. All rights reserved.

This is a work of fiction. All of the characters, names, incidents, organizations, and dialogue in this novel are either the products of the author's imagination or are used fictitiously.

WestBow Press books may be ordered through booksellers or by contacting:

WestBow Press
A Division of Thomas Nelson & Zondervan
1663 Liberty Drive
Bloomington, IN 47403
www.westbowpress.com
1 (866) 928-1240

Because of the dynamic nature of the Internet, any web addresses or links contained in this book may have changed since publication and may no longer be valid. The views expressed in this work are solely those of the author and do not necessarily reflect the views of the publisher, and the publisher hereby disclaims any responsibility for them.

Any people depicted in stock imagery provided by Thinkstock are models, and such images are being used for illustrative purposes only.
Certain stock imagery © Thinkstock.

ISBN: 978-1-9736-0064-0 (sc)
ISBN: 978-1-9736-0063-3 (e)

Library of Congress Control Number: 2017913597

Print information available on the last page.

WestBow Press rev. date: 11/7/2017

To my family and the lovely friends
who made childhood a delight

Contents

Acknowledgements ix
Preface xi

Treasures

The Rope Swing 1
Candle Making 9
The Annual Library Carnival 15
Cardboard as wearable art 22
The cardboard multiplex 26
The water marker 28

Winter among the Mountains

Rainville Ski Hill 33
Tucking 36
The Jungfrau T-bar 41
Etnas 47

Summer Camp Adventures

Lac Antoine 55
Turtle Races 56
Spy 60

The Garlic bread 65
The Far Dock 72
The sanctuary sound system 78
Swimming lessons 81
Ibex and amethyst 87
Pennies on the tracks 94

Albin

Albin 99
Albin and Hanna's Backyard Garden 104
Albin and the harmonica 112
Albin and the daily walk 115

The Great Outdoors

Spa day 121
Camping with Black Bears 127
The Bare Bear and the Hospital 134
The slip and slide 137

Epilogue 145

Acknowledgements

Thank you to those anonymous gems who inspired these stories, my mom for encouraging me to write, my father, who is an inspiration himself, the publishing team at WestBow Press, and to my Editor, Sandra Mcintyre and her neighbour 'Rolo' who made 'The Village that Raised Us' a reality

Preface

JOY, LOVE AND LAUGHTER ARE a natural part of our lives. They aren't always found in the big, boisterous and momentous. The elements of life that make us the happiest are so often the small moments we hardly pause to notice and yet cherish our entire adult lives.

This selection of stories celebrates the everyday, those moments between the first day of school and going to university, when children, play, make friends, learn skills, and are filled with a natural wonder of the world. *The Village That Raised Us* is a celebration of joy and life. It is a celebration of the love and laughter of Ana, Samuel, Nina, Lione and Benjamin, growing up in the imaginary small Swiss village of 'Pluie.' Rainville.

I hope their adventures will make you laugh, smile, pause, and feel inspired as you also create happiness and live your moments in love, just as these children did.

Treasures

The Rope Swing

Mystery creates wonder and wonder is the basis of man's desire to understand.
- Neil Armstrong

OF ALL THE TREASURES OF youth, for one brief moment of summer, the rope swing excels as the best of the old adventure ground. Two of the older kids from the neighborhood lead Ana to it, brushing back trees and brush and unveiling the secret as one would sweep aside the curtain of a priceless artifact or miraculous flying invention located on the edge of a woody cliff.

The dense foliage of forest branches that stretch out their needles into the plain air above a steep descent diffuses the bright sunshine of the August day. It is a drop so much like a cliff that one might actually call it that. Ana raises an eyebrow and stares upward at her companions. As Ana gazes up at the majestic Nadalbaum and then outwards into the void in awe, watching silently, the boys laugh while gauging her response intently. There, tied to one of the higher branches of the pine, on the edge of the cliff, is a sturdy, knotted rope. It looks, well, a little precarious.

She stands on her tiptoes, reaching with outstretched palms into the emptiness towards the rope, which edges away coyly, barely within grasping distance. Her runners shift in the dirt a bit. A pebble slides from the ledge in a bouncing freefall, tumbling downward, gaining air, rolling, and then bouncing again before sinking into the branches of a fir with a happy shudder.

There are slide marks where larger runners have slid and scuffle marks from kids attempting their re assent. Overall, however, the rope has a sturdy look and represents the great fun of flight. The older kids, delighting in their treasure, set about making Ana solemnly promise supreme neighbourhood secrecy. This is the kind of secret meant for sharing. In fact, it is the kind of secret meant for sharing solely with other kids.

First, one must learn how to swing. A crash course on tree-branch swinging includes: how to run, how to grasp the higher knot with both hands, and then how to allow one's feet or bottom to rest securely on the lower knot while simultaneously flying out and around the tree. She hesitates, sitting in the soft earth. Her face pointing upwards curiously as the others enthusiastically take turns. They glide, almost effortlessly, as their bodies soar, suspended mid air in a wide arc. One kid after the other lands safely, their feet thunking on the leeward side of the tree's trunk. To Ana's delight, after a few minutes the older kids decide that she is indeed brave enough and worthy of learning to do the same.

At dinner that night, Ana shows her gratitude and loyalty by keeping the secret. She responds to the inevitable amiable question period with a simple and general statement about her day's activities.

"What did you learn today?" her father asks, transferring Brussels sprouts from his plate to hers when her mother's eyes are averted elsewhere.

Ana eagerly skewers her favourite vegetables rolling around the beige and blue everyday dinnerware and rapidly recalls a lesson learned at school. Do her parents know that the planets Venus and Mars are named after the Roman gods of love and war? And that Venus rotates in a clockwise direction, counter to the other planets?

It isn't so much about the secret, she *usually* shares every adventure, every activity; however, children of that age intuit what adults may not understand. Thank goodness he hadn't pressed with, "What did you *do* today?"

After dinner, the Loocke family arrives and Ana ushers them upstairs, where in excited whispers she shares the secret of her newfound play space. Solemnly and eagerly she dispenses this local kid wealth with Samuel, Nina, Lione and Benjamin, her close pals, only after having drawing from each of them the promise to respect the elder kids' secret habitat in return.

These four, the band of eager adventurers about to share in the treasure of a secret world at the edge of the neighbouring cul-de-sac, set out the following day to find the rope swing. Ana and Samuel, the oldest, followed by Nina and Lione. The youngest, Benjamin, not yet old enough to join them, stays at home with his mom as the rest of the troupe adventure.

The day presents itself as sunny, with a hint of a breeze. Upon arriving, the rope swing glows keenly at the edge of the dirty, rugged cliff. The kids looked at it as one would the lost ark of the covenant or the Holy Grail. Ana and her crew are the Indiana Joneses stumbling upon the lost city, entering the padded enchanted circle around the old pine tree with curiosity, eagerness and trepidation.

Within a few minutes they are taking in the potentially devastating plunge. Old growth trees grow well here, their roots more or less wrapping around the cliff on the steep and almost impossible cliff face. Below, well below, and hidden from view by the density of pine foliage, is the frog pond, a magical place teaming with life. The earth below is damp, acrid and the almost black-red colour of aromatic humus. This place is majestic, picturesque enough of a scene to lull the young into accepting the implicit challenge offered by the rope, cliff and tree. Directly out from the edge Ana and the Loocke family kids can see the clear expanse of blue sky punctuated softly by the deep green of pines.

After careful inspection it is deemed by the committee of children that the quotient of adventure and fun exceed the obvious danger. Ana, having studied the process the day before, is self selected as the one most capable of introducing them to the practical world of rope swinging. She elected to fly first. She grasps hold of the rope with both hands and, with a little run at it, takes a flying leap outwards. Her feet leave solid ground as she soars gracefully into the nothingness of pure air, swinging in a perfect arc around the tree and then back onto the solid ground of the tree's northern side. Her feet land with a thunk, sliding slightly on the soft earth beneath. Somehow she maintains her poise despite wavering and on landing, manages to straighten just enough to assure her companions that, yes, perhaps this is safe enough. A chorus of young voices cheers.

Of course, in the days to come, there are several near misses. These are tense moments when children are left dangling precariously above the cliff edge as the rescue ensues. Friends' bodies stretch from the precipice, arms, hands and fingers straining and extending to reach a toe, ankle or piece of rope. Kids leaping with too little energy find themselves stranded above the abyss. They call out as tree branches are held out to them so as to snag a tangible bit of body or rope and bring the friend's dangling self back to safety before arm muscles grow weary.

There are two options to recovery: the first is for other kids to rescue the stranded; the second is releasing the rope and grasping the lower knot while lowering one's body gingerly. This is followed by leaping upward and inward towards the cliff face. All this is done while hoping to land softly with minimal downward slippage as one's feet and full body plant shakily in the soft, spongy dirt or springy branches of a nearby tree.

The latter option, lowering oneself and then leaping inward towards the cliff face, is a bit messier. It delays the children's fun for several minutes as companions cheer and encourage the person dragging themselves back up the incline. There are the pine needles and mud on hands to contend with. Then, on tiptoe, with the most upper body strength one can muster, the goal is to raise oneself above the precipice to firm ground, as if a climber completing the last section of a particularly dirty and grueling climb.

After the discovery of the rope swing, the days and weeks shone brightly, that is, until the day came when the parents uncovered the kids' treasure. This came after one of the younger, braver ones, with shorter arms and legs, missed the arc a little and lost grip of the rope. A catastrophic event was most fortunately averted as the child had his tumble broken by tree branches and shrubbery. So, our little hero returned home with bruises, bloodied knees, elbows and back, torn clothing and the most outrageous story of harrowing survival.

That was the day the parents caught wind of the source of the children's mysterious daily absences and learned that this new favourite pastime could dangerously and easily propel or plunge any one of their children into the bone-breaking abyss.

On the day of discovery a little parent-huddle forms. The children gather around their parents in the Andrews' living room. There is the hush of voices and tones of concern. Parents begin the entertainment vs danger assessment, gauging the risks. Neighbours arrive with comments. Then the troupe, parents in tow, make the five-or seven-minute walk from their living room across the road and into the forest to this enchanted play area. Jacob and Mark choose to "assess" by "testing," an amusing and courageous process that involves tugging on the rope to observe its strength and peering up into the branches as Ana had done. They assess the trajectory by swinging on the rope, looking down into the abyss as they soar in mid air, then, looking back up to the "safe" landing. The looking down part does everyone in.

"Always keep your eyes on the landing," suggests Ana feebly as the parents land, wobbly. Jacob dusts the dirt from his slacks and glances up at the rope again. They repeat the process "for good measure." Each parent takes a turn.

The parents more or less have the grace of their children, but a good deal more *chutzpah* than expected. The kids look at each other with muted admiration and amusement while Jacob and Mark feign 'parental' concern, barely hiding the grins on their faces.

No one ever knows who removed the knotted rope from its perch, though it must have been quite the task. Someone would have had to climb up the tree and untie the rope. The parents kept *that* secret to themselves. And so, the tree and its environment return to their former normality. The rope vanishes without a trace, kids return to bikes, basketballs and fort making, and the tiny piece of surrounding forest, though always enchanting, loses its particular wonder.

Candle Making

> *Thousands of candles can be lighted from a single candle, and the life of the candle will not be shortened. Happiness never decreases by being shared.*
>
> —Buddha

THE FIFTY-POUND BAG OF BEESWAX in the basement emanated an aura of timeless kitchen adventures. It spoke of dedicated youth and Swiss pastures and it spoke of the family of beekeepers Ana's father Jacob met during his more adventurous and restless phase, the exploratory years when Jacob travelled the country and the world before settling into family life with Hanna and Ana. From the bottom of the stairs, standing pertly beside shelves filled with jars of pickles, peaches, pears, and raspberry jam was the coarse gunny sack. The sack held large golden chunks of rugged and aromatic beeswax which, until it was depleted nearly ten years later, was the source of the yearly holiday tradition of candle making.

Once a year, the magic of candle making unfolds, as

large pieces of the aromatic raw material are drawn up from the basement and the modest, middle-class kitchen transforms into a family-renowned candle-making shop full of the scents and sounds of an authentic studio. Water boiling on the stove in massive canning pots as Mason jars bob lightly, shimmering with warmly melted wax. The kids' faces glowing with anticipation as the solid wax slowly melts into a nearly translucent golden liquid. Wicks are prepared by tying a small weight to a string from a roll purchased at the local general store and laying them out in tidy rows all ready for dipping. Next, doweling bits, brought up from the garage, are fastened above the stove to be hung with candles at various stages of growth. At some point during the process, someone inevitably thinks of playing Christmas music or classical music, and the cheery sound of it fills the air from the living room.

Soon, kitchen windows steam up with warmth and the entire house achieves a festive, cottage feeling.

If you haven't done this yourself, the candle-making process itself is relatively simple and enchanting. The wax melts. You dip the string, then remove it to cool. Once the wax has cooled sufficiently, another layer of wax is added and the process is repeated until the candle is of a satisfactory width or will no longer grow. Then, the bottom is trimmed and cooled before the candles are set aside on the old oak table and finally wrapped as gifts or stored for family use. Lighting a homemade beeswax candle holds a special charm. When lit, the final product fills the home with the delightful scent of sweet, air-purifying beeswax and the sparkle of candlelight.

As with any craft, it's in the details where the love is

found. Finding the Goldi-locks temperature of the heated wax is imperative. Overheat the vessel and the candle cannot grow. The result? When a candle is dipped, the hot wax melts the former layers of cooled wax, leaving a fledgling candle empty and the candle maker holding a bare string. A thermometer assists; however, even so, overheated bare strings happen on several occasions before the perfect temperature is discovered. The same is true of an under-heated, sticky jar of cooling liquid. Too much viscosity and the cooling liquid will adhere to smaller, cold particles, creating clumps as the mass begins to accumulate. These cling to the thin candle, causing a lumpy appearance. This bumpiness can sometimes be smoothed out after several applications of wax; however, clumpy wax inevitably interferes with the smoothness of the final product.

Each year, Hanna and the kids worked on perfecting their art, and a kind of assembly line naturally formed amongst family members and guests. Hanna manned the heating of the wax, Ana and Jessica prepared the wicks, Jacob brought snacks, and so on. Each individual served an important role in a process punctuated by laughter, story-telling and snacks. Homemade snacks shared the stage, and the symbology of shared nourishment enveloped them in motherly love.

Somehow, snacks are something taken to their highest form in the Andrews home. At every gathering, formal or casual, Hanna produces fruits, veggies, cheeses and homemade chocolates, cookies, and of course the essential, trail mixture. Hanna's family trail mix recipe is a mainstay at every and all of these family gatherings, so that one can hardly tell whether the family gathered to create or indulge.

This isn't true of only the Christmas candle season; basically every day is a celebration worthy of delicious treats baked up in the family kitchen.

Hanna plays the classics of Mozart or Simon and Garfunkel, stringing each string carefully as each individual candlette on its way to becoming a candle is attached to the doweling between dipping. Layer after layer is added patiently. As soon as a certain candle reaches the desired width, or can take no more wax, it is set aside to dry on a doweling rack hung above the sink and another is begun.

Year after year, the beauty and magic of this process is injected with creativity. Of course, the process grows old after several years and so the phase of creative expansion began. What else can they make, Hanna and her little group of eager nestlings ask themselves, bright faces staring into the glowing jars of melted wax. And that is when the adventure begins. Nina, her companions and Hanna search the house to find vessels to use as a worthy candle holder. It becomes a treasure hunt. Who can find the most beautiful, the most useful, the most unusual. After several minutes, hours or sometimes days, they return with arms full of jars, glue and found objects such as construction paper, feathers, macaroni or shells – glitter is banned (although it isn't entirely unfound) in the house following an incident involving a glue gun, a snug lid, and an exploding glitter container.

Sometimes Ana makes experimental sculptural pieces or fingers sculptures of wax, using her hands and fingers as the mold. Warm wax, when it isn't so warm that it scalds long slender fingers and hands, shows the finest of details.

A tattered old Sunday school crafts book, found in a

Tupperware storage container yields the knowledge that one can create a jar that looks a little like real stained glass simply by painting a plain, clear jar with transparent acrylic paint and then filling it with wax and wick or with a small tea light. Every one of the Andrews loved ones has received small, hand-painted Mason jars glued with buttons, string and shells for at least one Christmas, along with a handwritten letter and also a note from Mom and Dad.

After years of candle production, only once did this process end in disaster. You can't say that Ana and her old friend Jen weren't warned. They were. In fact they first encountered the idea of homemade honey and wax facial masks from the cautionary story in the paperback storybook *In Grandma's Attic* where Arleta, the 19th century main character and her friend, children much like Ana and Jen although from a much earlier era, read a recipe of ingredients lacking amounts from a glossy magazine. Erringly, the young Arleta mixes the wrong proportions of honey and wax together, a mixture, which when applied as a facial mask results in a sticky, gooey mess and the removal of which leaves the girls with sore, raw and red skin.

"Those who cannot remember history are condemned to repeat it," said Winston Churchill, and, apparently, so are some who do.

Most people would say Ana and Jen were bright girls . . . and yet, the wisdom inherent in this story's moral was overshadowed by the enticing suggestion that one could make a facial of the proper proportions of honey and beeswax. The idea was reasonable after all.

"I know the problem," declared Ana to her dearest friend one evening as they tidied up after candle making.

"It's the proportions. We could do it properly. We'll just add less honey and more wax. "

The wax was cooling, light and gooey on the stove, and the table was laden with beeswax candles dipped, trimmed and laid out. There were also painted jars of golden liquid cooling and a finger sculpture or two after a day of creating. The light had faded when Ana and Jessica, almost ready to clean up, began just one more project.

"They say that if you do it right, it removes blemishes."

Dad gave them a wary eyebrow and retreated to the living room with his newspaper and a cup of hot tea. Ana and Jen didn't really have blemishes. However, whatever these blemishes were, Ana knew she didn't want them on her nose, and this remedy promised to make her skin soft and radiant. So Jen and Ana donned aprons once again, drew out some of the transparent melted wax and began.

"This much honey, and this much wax."

It was an intuitive, unmeasured process. The result *looked* tame enough.

Are you surprised to learn that they did use the wrong proportions? The girls were slightly more successful than their storybook counterparts. They did in fact create a reasonable facial, one resulting in laughter as opposed to tears. However, one couldn't say that it worked either. That was the day Jen and Ana learned that the skin takes twenty-eight days to regenerate and for months afterward, Ana wasn't quite sure that the sheen had left her nose and brow completely.

The Annual Library Carnival

> *You have to learn the rules of the game. And then you have to play better than anyone else.*
>
> -Unknown

SUMMER ALWAYS ARRIVES AS A surprise to the residents of Rainville. Winter lasts and lasts, and then spring lasts and lasts, and suddenly, summer. Almost as though without notice the melts snow and chirping robins give way to what feels like two months or so of reasonable warmth as the little mountain town basks in the sunshine, and the dry, dusty roads of summer bring festivals, fundraisers, carnivals and derbies.

There are roller derbies, the annual parade, Rainville Antler days, and, best of all, in the Andrews family, the annual public library carnival. Hanna volunteers at the library. She, Annabel and Bess plan everything. She loves to cheerlead and promote the "best summer celebration there is." Officially, the library carnival is staged to raise money towards the purchase of new books. In reality Annabel and

Bess just love a good, old-fashioned carnival. Of course, the library has a presence at the other festivals also! The annual parade is one of them. One year, the team of librarian, library assistant and Hanna came up with a barnyard theme for the parade, and since no one else would do it, they dressed Ana up like a pig in a fuzzy pink costume and snout. They handed her a basket of hard candies to toss at, er, *to*, delighted on-lookers comprised partially of teasing friends who ran along side of the float shouting and oinking with their hand held out as the float drifted along the main road.

"Oinker!" Samuel called in his classic ribbing style as he waved at her, running along-side the float. Ana looked ahead. Her father, who had the tripod set up just ahead of them, was smiling encouragingly and waving as Samuel continued shouting "I have the perfect picture to show at your wedding!"

"That's enough," whispered Annabel gently, brushing back woolly sheep ears and covering Ana's basket with her sheep hoof as she nodded towards the other side of the street. "Toss them gently and perhaps those other kids would like some candy," said Annabel with a smile.

By the time the slow-moving float reached him, Mr. Andrews snapped an image of Ana sitting politely and waving like a pink pork belle in a fuzzy oversized onsie.

As exciting as the annual parade is, the Carnival fundraiser, however, is the library's own.

This carnival is a highlight of Hanna's summer. For years now, Hanna has enjoyed volunteering at the library. She sorts returns, re-shelves, and checks in and out well-loved, dog-eared books of the public collection twice a week, on Tuesdays and Thursdays. The community she has developed around cheery and chubby Bess the librarian, Annabel the librarian assistant, and herself flourishes, and for months now, the librarians and library volunteers have planned and organized, calling on community members until it seemed as though everyone in town was drawn into the celebration and compelled to contribute or compete. Everyone in town loves a good summer carnival.

The annual library festival is held in the arena. The local skating rink holds the smell of rubber mats and hockey equipment, which is what goes on one season of the year. Now, the smooth, iceless concrete floors provide a wide-open recreation space and the zamboni doors open to the outside, inviting a steady stream of people in and out either from there, the curling rink side, or the front doors. Someone related to Bess has access to carnival games and a popcorn maker, cotton candy spool, dunk tank, tricycle race track, and a fishing tank with plastic toys. Of course, there is face painting. Outside there are hotdogs in tinfoil bins cooked by the fire department, cake and Neapolitan ice cream buckets melting in coolers packed with ice.

The day of the festival arrives with bright, sunny weather and most of the town shows up, cheery faced with hotdogs in hand. Bess is grinning, busy stringing balloons and streamers from the top of a ladder. She's holding a handful of ribbons as her husband fills balloons with helium as quickly as she can pin them.

"Ana, darling, would you be a sweetie and run and grab me those push pins from the desk?" Bess calls, drawing the final pin from her apron pocket. This year, as Bess sizes up the number of volunteers, she determines they have the perfect number.

It is funny how short-lived perfection is sometimes. So, perhaps it is better to say that, at first, they had the perfect number. Actually, they had the perfect number until they discovered, too late, that the line for tossing at the dunk tank was drawn a bit too short.

It wasn't one of the first things they noticed. The doors opened promptly to a string of eager friends and family who had been helping to set up so this little detail was missed at the moment.

Other moments are happening. Hanna and her husband are pouring a massive bag of sugar into the cotton candy spinner and discussing the potential quantities needed to successfully provide for the day, just as the first eager kids peek around the door and enter with their parents. Annabel tapes nametags when the first three "volunteers" land, in the water, one after another.

Kirsplash!, Kirsplash!, Whoosh!

The three happen to be: the fire chief, the librarian's husband and a neighbour of Annabel's. These three also happen to be the *only* three signed up to volunteer at the dunk tank that day. Fortunately, all but Annabel's neighbour were good sports. Mysteriously, a home-baked pie arrived at her door a few days later and that's when things smoothed out again.

Hanna inched the tape a meter back and tested it with her best softball arm. Then Jacob tested it. Better.

Bess, realizing they are a body short only a moment after all three "dunkies" retire to drink coffee and change amidst chatter and good natured ribbing, calls upon Ana to assist.

"How would you like to paint faces for an hour?" she asks with the robust maternal authority of a seasoned grandparent looking directly into Ana's hesitant eyes. Well, at least she hadn't been asked to sit in the dunking station!

Now, as you can imagine, there is only one way to answer such a request, and soon enough, Ana, talented painter or not, is seated on a little stool with a folding white plastic table of face-painting crayons and dipping paints laid out in front of her. The first child, a sweet girl with curly black hair standing with her mother, is lined up and easily transformed into a butterfly, one wing on each cheek and the antenna above the bridge of her nose. The second child became Spiderman, or rather the web Spiderman would have used, black crayon dipping and linking like webbing. The third is a little trickier.

"Make me the Hulk."

A green crayon solved that quickly enough, much to the delight of the bulky kid and to the slight dismay of his mother, who had dressed him in a white cotton golf shirt. He walked away grinning and wiping his chin with his shoulder as his mother glanced furtively back at the painting station. As word spreads, the line grows, and Ana's skills grow exponentially as she learns to make the most of her live canvases, painting a smudgy rainbow, a blue star, Strawberry Shortcake and so on.

Of course, an hour turns into two. Painting was fun at first, but soon she runs out of ideas. She is confidently dabbing at an oval of red with a black paintbrush, adding the dots to a ladybug, when Samuel comes along, Samuel, the classic prankster. Samuel, who made fun of her at the parade. That's when Ana comes up with a Herculean trick so perfect it is almost accidental.

"Samuel, this is so much fun!" She said, her eyes

laughing but without changing her tone enough to arouse suspicion. "Would you like to do it for while, while I buy us some cotton candy?"

Samuel, wise and hard to fool, grins knowingly. This isn't about squirming his way out, this is about negotiating the best possible terms.

"Cotton candy and a fishing game token?" he barters, and then, just like Atlas shifting the world onto his shoulder, there he was, Samuel, holding the crayons at an angle as he tilts his head and squints at the next kid in line, a kid who is requesting to be painted into a Transformer.

Now Samuel is the face painter and Ana is free. She threads her way through the crowd to the public washrooms and then, basking in the adventures of the day, proceeds to the cotton candy line, where her father is elbow deep in the pink confection. Working the gauzy candy around a paper cone with the adept flourish one could only image of a seasoned coal miner, he is just a little more than that. Ana looks around the pleasantly full summer rink. She isn't certain whether to return directly, she is free after all, and the fishing wall had yet to be fished. Perhaps she is thinking of the adventures waiting if she doesn't return, at least not immediately. The line threads forward. Maybe she'll just go to the park and have a swing on the swing and then eat a hotdog. She glances over at Samuel, who is just putting the finishing touches on a wrinkle dog, or was it a bear?

The sweet taste of freedom lasts little longer than the line-up for cotton candy. That's when Hanna, who had been taking tickets at the dunk tank, is convinced to dunk, and is dunked, on the third or fourth ball toss by the volunteer firefighter and his fellow ski patroller from across the cul-de-sac. And as soon as you know it, Bess is beckoning to Ana again. Hanna, wrapped safely and warmly in a fireman's blanket, goes home to change and return.

And there it is, Ana manning the dunk tank.

"Try your best," she says to a line of ball throwers, delighted to have a warm and dry task on the outside of the netting, having skillfully avoided the "wet seat" as they called it.

She hands three balls to Nina and deposits the ten-dollar bill into the black portable cash box. Nina sports a glittery, smudgy rainbow on her cheek. Taking aim, the first ball lands a bit short and rolls the remaining foot to its destination below the brightly painted bull's-eye. The second slams into the nets above the planks and the third narrowly misses.

"How often do people actually dunk?" called the robust, ruddy-faced mining man in line next.

Nina just grins, taking his money as Brian, her neighbour's companion and fellow volunteer firefighter takes his seat above the tank. He adjusts himself on rickety chair and, leaning forward, answers her with a grin of his own.

"Do your best, Mike. If you toss that ball the way you did a baseball last Tuesday, I'm safe."

Cardboard as wearable art

Hitch your wagon to a star.
                    - Ralph Waldo Emerson

WHERE DO FUN AND ADVENTURE come from? To Samuel and Ana, these come from a myriad of places. Perhaps the source of inspiration is in a cart of apples or oranges from the general store or grocer, or in the form of a package from the mailbox.

In Rainville, adventure often arrives by post. The daily pilgrimage of retrieving the mail from the rural post office provides excitement in itself and is so often the source of adventure. Rainville's mail delivery system doesn't offer door-to-door service. There aren't enough people to do that. One has to retrieve it themselves. In the Andrews household, this is a daily adventure undertaken with the precision of clockwork precisely a few minutes after Jacob returned from work and prior to dinner. Jacob and Hanna, and sometimes the entire family, Ana and Albin, the mutt, bundle into the comfy blue Renault and drive to the rural shopping square. Often the chill of the winter air outside the car and distance allow time to trace the outline of trees, smiling faces or a tent on the steaming windows with one's fingertips.

Arriving, they enter the mall, a charmingly constructed stone structure, the floor a ruddy stone rectangle. The white roof, the brown ceramic tiled corridors smell faintly of bleach and humus. After calling a greeting to the baker from the Parisian style cafe and bakery, and visiting with this or that person, the Andrewses make their way to the post office. Everyone in Rainville knows them, and they know more or less everyone. That's just how it is in Rainville.

The clerk, a cheerful, pudgy woman with a broad smile and melodic voice, welcomes them with familiarity. A shiny chrome bell alerts her from her work in the back and forward she comes. A delivery notice is handed to her. There is a moment's pause, as she hustles to the back shelves to bring forward the taped and sealed bundle. As many times as there are packages, Ana's eyes always grow wide with anticipation and she is rarely disappointed. Sometimes the delivery is books, or other times gifts from grandparents who live in St. Tropez. There's something magical about cardboard isn't there? The Andrewses bring their deliveries home and unwrap them with anticipation, and then, when the interiors had been explored and unwrapped, the appropriate thank-you letter written or phone call to grandma placed, the box itself becomes the muse.

Ahh, the fun of a cardboard box. It presents a building material with so many of possibilities. And so it is that this group of kids may leave bikes and water guns strewn on the lawn, and every sort of indoor toy in the toy boxes at the moment of the delivery of a new appliance. Children, who can recollect spending hours in imaginary play under tables and sheets designed as tents and covered in blankets, or days in their forest "homes," are truly blessed. So it is with the Andrewses and Loockes. Such is the joy of the cardboard box.

The beauty of such a building material as a cardboard box is this: This humble form has sturdy plain brown walls that present themselves as a blank slate for a fascinating array of creations; one can cut and reshape them or leave them as they are. They are strong enough to hold weight and shape, and the clean, plain walls are the perfect conduit for a myriad of crafting materials. Repurposing cardboard is a delightful craft and one in which the kids find endless hours of fascination.

The year the Loockes and Andrewses formed wearable cars of apple crates as Halloween costumes was a highlight of the school costume parade. Ana was too shy to bring such a bulky contraption to school and wound up parading around in leotards, sweater and an apologetic smile, much to the embarrassment of her parents, who thought the car was "her best costume yet." Samuel and Nina did wear theirs, and won the annual elementary school costume contest hands down.

How was the box itself transformed into a wearable vehicle? This was achieved by removing the bottom from the sturdy apple crate boxes and then fitting these around the abdomen so that one's torso, head and neck could be seen above the windshield. They then firmly fastened these to their shoulders with twine and set about the task of constructing functioning steering wheels wrapped in tin foil. Of course, the absolute crowning achievement was a working hood and boot with folding hinges so that one could open or close them adeptly to store Halloween booty. Inside hood and boot were stowed plastic grocery bags or pillow cases as candy receptacles in both the front and back to ensure an even weight.

They weren't quite done, however. Vehicles need headlights, and these were made with black marker after which a grill was applied using a combination of tin foil and a glue gun. As you can imagine, this endeavour filled the entire basement with crafting materials and children for days and days prior to the Halloween season as they took great care to perfect each and every detail prior to the final day.

Halloween came with a deep and magical dump of pillowy snow. Ana and Samuel donned their snowsuits and costumes and headed out to trick-or-treat. That year, each succeeded in filling the boot and hood bags with Halloween treats twice as they made their rounds to several neighbourhoods beyond the usual circuit. The weather was pleasantly crisp, and newly fallen snow of the mountain village piled high, glistening as they tromped on their rounds.

Rumour has it that one or two of the boys made the rounds twice, though that was never confirmed. The kids had such a stash of licorice, mini chocolate bars, tootsie rolls, Mocken, ring pops, and such in the coat closet that it lasted for months. They swapped the premium mini Lindts with one another and a lunch recesses until at least August of that year.

The cardboard multiplex

> *I dwell in Possibility -*
> *A fairer House than Prose -*
>   -Emily Dickinson

OF COURSE, BOXES AREN'T ONLY wearable fashion. From such mundane treasures as a new refrigerator or dryer crates are born a world unto itself. To the little troupe, always in search of adventure, the day the Loockes purchased a fridge, dish washer, washing machine and dryer stands out as a special day. Unpacking them from enormously large, study boxes is as magical as a second Christmas in spring. Their parents talk upstairs about the various qualities and capacities of the stove, fridge and dryer and washer. The kids vie to possess the boxes themselves. Once procured, they parade them into the flat, empty area of the basement, divvy them up, then un-divvy, and, working together on a single project, soon find themselves immersed in the domestic and enchanted world of kids, homes and castles.

Empowered with felt markers, crayons, a box cutter, glue, tape and bits of fabric, these enchanted builders soon transformed their otherwise mundane materials into a towering village of castles. This is a cumulative effort, building in a shared partnership with the pure enthusiasm of those who love and delight in creating. The buildings are joined together with tunnels, doors and secret entrances. The exteriors are decorated with paint, coloured and glued and the interiors made bright and cheerful with blanket tapestries and all manner of pillows and other nesting materials.

For several days, if not weeks, they played and played in a world lost beyond time. At first, they were so engrossed it the task, in fact, that Samuel's mom Mary rolled her eyes gently, pointing out that there is also a world called "outside." She was forced to request that the kids at a minimum pause to have granola bars and juice when they refused lunch. They took such enthusiasm in their task that it took Hanna calling Ana home for dinner to eventually draw a pause, until another day.

The water marker

> *To practice five things under all circumstances constitutes perfect virtue; these five are gravity, generosity of soul, sincerity, earnestness, and kindness.*
>
> - Confucius

ANA IS A FORTUNATE CHILD. Her neighbours are lovely, good-natured people and she adores them. Although she doesn't always bond with them, or spend hours catching frogs in the pond, picking raspberries or creating as she does with her family and dearest companions, neighbours of Ana's age offer the friendly presence of a generally cohesive village at an age where all are welcome and most are cherished. Of all the neighbourly acquaintances, Pietro and his elder brothers bring the most amusement. They are also most often in trouble. Fortunately, however, at that age at least, it is the laughable kind of trouble people enjoy. The family lived near, sharing her avenue as a child. When they were older, they all moved to houses within a few blocks of each other. The eldest accompanied her father in building a garden fence one summer. Every weekend, for weeks and months he arrived in the yard early to help Jacob as he prepared mortar, stones and wood. The Andrews family felt tremendous gratitude as that year was also the year Jacob broke his wrist and the extra labour provided a tremendous assistance. Provided a tremendous assistance.

Pietro had a knack for getting himself into predicaments so outrageous that one couldn't help but remember them for years to come. Like the time in elementary school when he arrived at school with large splotches of blue and green food colouring inked on his face, neck and arms. Such a bright and vivid blue and green that it looked as though artist Jackson Pollack had used his face as a canvas on which to paint "shimmering substance."

At eight or so, he was already a curiously tough and tumble kid, actually quite sensitive. He missed two days of elementary school due to his face-paint predicament before his mother, who'd scrubbed Pietro's face and arms with soap and rough cloth both days to no avail, gently required him to return to class. At school, his presence was missed. The kids called out to him, gathering around in a little circle. Then of course there was the question of the blue and green ink splotches. This precipitated a deep blush, nearing eclipsing his freckles and turning the blue splotches on his cheeks a dark purple as he explained that his brothers and he had invented the ingenious plan to indicate which of them had won the recent water fight.

All kids in small towns have water pistols, and most have super-soakers, water fights being a tradition of summer. Ana and the Loockes have epic battles lasting days and involving all manner of implements: the usual water balloons, as well as buckets, tubs tied with string (this usually backfired on the person "rigging" the tub), sprinklers and the garden hose. Hanna draws the line at garden hoses despite the indoor kitchen sink having the most magnificent squirter hose you could possibly imagine. The indoor squirter hose remains strictly out of bounds and because of the outdoor hoses only rule, respectfully, is used only in the direst of "emergencies."

The day before Pietro arrived at school after his green- and blue-inking began with an ordinary case of creative problem solving: You see the problem, he explained, is that during a water fight everyone gets wet. When everyone is blasted and soaking, it is extremely hard to tell who has won a water challenge. The solution, as they saw it at the time, was for him and his brothers to add food colouring to the water. Red, blue, green, one colour each. In this way they could tally up the number of direct squirts and tell who had won. This was a genius idea! Briefly, Ana wondered why she hadn't thought of it! A moment later, the awful truth arrived suddenly, like the freight train of realization, and she could do nothing but stare in pure awe and horror, a twinkle in her eye as she desperately tried to show the appropriate emotion upon understanding that Pietro's face wouldn't return to its normal freckly pinkishness the next day, or the next or even the day after that. This was because blue and green food colouring in that particular concentration, as it turns out, is pretty much permanent. It was about a month before Pietro reclaimed normal skin pigmentation, though frankly it seemed much longer for him. Oddly enough, his delegated colour was red, and, as most recalled, his brothers looked reasonably unscathed.

Winter among the Mountains

Rainville Ski Hill

THE SKI HILL, A BELOVED fixture of Rainville, hosts a moderate T-bar lift and a handful of runs. It is staffed primarily by dedicated and warm-hearted volunteers and fuelled on the passion and love of the sport. Rainville ski hill was born long after the village. Near old herding routes from high pasture, routes treaded down by goatherds and shepherds from local forests millennia before, more recently, an area was cleared, brushed and landscaped by the hard work and efforts of the town's enthusiast population. According to the local website, it was several decades after Ernst Gustav Constam, a Zurich engineer invented the T-bar in the late 1920s and began producing them in 1934, that the T-bar was installed. From the beginning, the ski hill has been a community passion. Today, the main "groomsman," also called Gustav, and his wife are particularly cherished and loved as dedicated Rainville enthusiasts. He is the first person grooming after a fresh powder has fallen and the last after an icy storm. There are only two lanes open to night skiing with the remaining seven open to skiers on weekends. Since the town is small, skiing is a popular diversion and many of the townspeople ski and socialize after school or work on the two, lit night runs.

Of the group, Ana joined the ski patrol first, egged on by older members of the ski community. This was almost accidental. She had happened to volunteer as a patient during the ski patrol's annual patient recovery training, bumping along in the sled behind patrollers in uniform. The lead patroller, who was a younger colleague of her father, seemed to be emphasising speed of recovery rather than patient safety. He zoomed down the hill as though doing slalom for the national Olympic team. Ana survived. Afterwards she was invited and joined ski patrol as a junior patroller, promptly receiving the nickname "blue crush."

Ski patrol offered her a free year of skiing whenever she liked. This rare treat gives young people the chance to learn first aid and to ski a season free in exchange for patrolling the hill once or twice a week, and of course access to the hill any other day. The training involves an intensive Seilbahnen Schweiz A-course, first aid instruction with a minimum eighty-five percent passing grade, another perk of the job. Since skiers are adept and rarely in need of a ski patrol service, the role of junior ski patrol is mainly a supportive one. During the several years Ana volunteered with the ski patrol, her only real call was to bandage the lip of a child hit by the T-bar. Although once, a pudgy kid from the neighbourhood around the school fell right in front of her. He did a stunt jump, then tumbled a good five yards, head over heels and sliding upside down for another several yards. Stunned, he lay in the snow long enough for Ana to assess, call her partner, and offer him a toboggan ride down. Caught up in the excitement, he pretended injury, which of course was mostly a bruised ego and the chance at a story Monday morning.

Jacob, Ana's father, joined with her the first year, partially with enthusiasm and partially to chaperone and protect the young adventurer. Almost immediately, he received the responsibility of scheduling the volunteer patrol staff and for several years the classic father-daughter duo became a mainstay on the Rainville slopes. Their enthusiasm was palpable and it was only a matter of a few seasons before Samuel and then Nina and her younger brothers joined the patrol, first as patrollers and then as lifties. With so many fabulous individuals to ski with, the group found skiing a delightful way to entertain themselves during these chilly mountain winters, and an almost inexhaustible reservoir of stories.

Tucking

> Miracles are a retelling in small letters of the very same story which is written across the whole world in letters too large for some of us to see.
>
> -C. S. Lewis

PIETRO AND HIS BROTHERS OFTEN frequent Rainville ski hill and so it is only natural that they also find themselves in pickles occasionally. A winding dirt road leads up to the Rainville ski hill where, at the base of the hill, stands a sturdy wooden structure known as the lodge. When Ana joined ski patrol as a teenager, the concrete basement of the lodge had already been constructed; however, mercifully, prior to that, the lodge is raised on stilts, with a shallow wide-open space of about a meter or so beneath, beyond which there is a steep embankment, a drop, and then the road below. In front of the lodge is a series of wooden ski stands for resting skis on while skiers enjoy hot chocolate or lunch inside. There is a plain or flat of a meter or so leading from the lodge up to these ski racks and this is where enthusiasts can stop at leisure to remove their skis in order to rendezvous indoors, or pause to adjust their bindings between runs. The hill itself begins a mere meters from the ski racks. This can become a somewhat precarious place, as the length of flat leading up to the ski racks, while adequate, is shorter than some. Most unlucky skiers, upon losing their balance or descending too quickly without having learned to stop properly . . . you see where I'm going with this, don't you? These hapless few find themselves careening into the mess of skiers and skis, usually with little consequence other than strewn skis and the laughter of observers. There was one time, however, when the ski racks and surrounding area were completely devastated, resulting in an area that looked somewhat like a band of trees that had been torn out of the ground and tossed in all directions after a tornado. It was Pietro who took the dubious honour and responsibility for this mishap.

The kids all love to race. Mastering the main route takes little effort and jumps and racing soon become the favourite challenge. Jumping had a brief popularity at first with the names used to describe the various jumps borrowed from Olympic freestyle ski jumping: the backscratcher, the spins, the front and back flips, the iron cross, and the grabs. The majority of kids mastered the most basic grabs and possibly a 180 or 360 at least before retiring to regular skiing or the more popular activity of racing. For Ana, retirement from jumping happened the day she missed landing a backscratcher and buried her skies "all the way to the boot, face first."

Samuel always raced *and* jumped, Nina never jumped, and Lione and Benjamin were speedy from the word "go." Racing was really what it was all about at that age. When it comes to racing they excel, egging each other on in friendly competition to see who can achieve the fastest time. Winning requires the im-plementation of the "tuck." Tucking is done by crouch-ing into a race position with arms and Poles to the side. Upon losing control or feeling wobbly, one is inclined, and often cautioned, to bale. While baling is prudent, it is ego bruising as it means either straightening and entering a series of S-turns intended to slow one's descent, or sinking sideways into the snow and ultimately wiping out. Wiping out comes in many forms. If the wipe out is massive, having involved either a great deal of speed or a particularly ungraceful bale, it inevitably becomes what is known as a "yard sale."

Yard sale: losing one's skis, poles and toque in a disarray of tumbling

The "yard sale" is discouraged. Racing rarely gets out of control and for the most part the overall group skill increases dramatically thanks to these kinds of games.

Were you wondering why I have faithfully described the lodge, on stilts, with its space beneath, the precarious ski rack situation, and shorter than average slowing area? Well, on this unfortunate day, the conditions were slightly faster and icier than would have been ideal for racing. The weather had warmed and then cooled and there had been little fresh snow the previous week, leading to a sheer, fast and unforgiving surface. Being the youngest of his brothers, Pietro often races the hardest so as to keep up and impress.

Perhaps he should have known to bale sooner. For whatever purpose, he doesn't. Now, he is racing with all he is worth, leaning in, alert to the positioning of himself in relation to fellow racers, and making tremendous speed when he whizzes by his brothers and fellow skiers. He *would* have gained great applause. He *would* have been hailed the day's hero and earned the respect of his cohort. He *would* have raised his hands in the air, elated.

It was hard to tell what exactly went wrong. Perhaps he focused on the route, or on looking behind him as he won the race. Perhaps he was imagining hot cocoa and accolades of admiring fans. He wasn't, you can be sure, aware of his presently awaiting . . . um, "situation." As you can imagine, it was at this point that he lost complete control of his speed and found himself in the dangerous situation of being stuck in permi-tuck.

Permi-tuck: the inability to stand from the tucking position while racing, usually alleviated only by falling and thus sliding into a stop.

So here he is in permi-tuck, unable to stand, slip or turn, and unwilling to fall. He comes barrelling down at such tremendous speed, somehow, with seemingly no awareness of this unfortunate situation except for that fleeting express on his face as if to say, "Oh No." Upon reaching the end of the track, he simply can't straighten as the ski rack comes closer and closer at a blinding rate, arriving with a *whoosh* and the tremendous sound of several pairs of skis colliding with each other as they take flight, then a *thunk* as they make contact with the snow, and then the rack, skis and, now, the flat area, is behind him.

Observers from the deck would have seen something resembling a blur and felt a moment of concern, as Pietro flew by them, or rather I should say, *towards* them, and then *under* them, barrelling between the ski racks before charging under the lodge, tucking lower (which functioned to increase his speed) to avoid the floorboards above, which he did only by millimetres, at which point he disappeared from view, landing several meters below on the dirt road miraculously whole and unscathed. They would have *heard* the collision.

Above, skiers were left staring at each other in wondrous disbelief, and at the scattered skis and poles strewn about, wondering about the new nickname, a nickname Pietro would hold for several years running: Tasmanian devil.

The Jungfrau T-bar

> *Keep your eyes on the stars, and your feet on the ground.*
> - Theodore Roosevelt

THE LARGER RESORT OF POWDERMOUNT near Rainville is spectacular. People around the world the world know where to find meters of fresh powder and many, many runs. There are challenges of life that bring us towards adulthood, little stages one achieves like learning to tie one's shoes, or the first day of elementary school, like learning to ride a bicycle or learning to ski and, for the kids growing up around Rainville, once you've learned to ski in Rainville, the only thing left after that is mastering the Jungfrau T-Bar on the upper flank of PowderMount. The Jungfrau T-Bar is the length of T-bar vertical from the chair lift to the top of the mountain. The Jungfrau T-bar is a notoriously and intentionally challenging narrow section of track. At the beginning, the track runs between dense trees and then, higher, deposits its fares at an altitude where there aren't any trees. Mastering the ascent separates the beginners from the pros, the kids from the seasoned skiers. To reach the top of the Jungfrau T-Bar is to be inducted into a world of powder, diamond runs and moguls. It is to have become a competent skier, and in the life of a seven, eight, or nine year old, this is massive.

Did I mention that the only thing standing between Samuel and Ana and a world of pristine powder and smooth, untracked slopes, between these two and black diamond runs and moguls, between the world of amateur skiers and experts is an almost impossibly steep vertical, and that the only way up is a tottery T-bar? That rickety little boomerang-shaped apparatus with springs, and a propensity to launch kids from its bar the way an elastic band hurls a wad of paper.

"If you can reach the top of the mountain via the T-bar, you can ski those routes," their parents would announce, smugly, checking their watches and alerting the kids to the location of the lunch station with the parental confidence of adults who know the abilities of their kids.

Every year, when milder runs had been run successfully and raced several times, they would turn their attention towards the Jungfrau T-bar. Season after season the ambitious and determined Samuel and Ana struggled. And every year until this one they . . . toppled . . . and had their snow pants filled with snow, and had their backs scratched by chunks of ice, and every year they bruised their arms before releasing the bar and hobbling into the ski hill, mid trail. More times than they could count, they found their faces dragging along cold billows of snow with their suspenders, or pockets caught on the bar, dragging them along as they scrambled to free themselves. And then there is the tumbling, and loss of skis, or poles, or mitts. This year, they promised themselves, this year would be different.

This year, recalling other years, the ski lifty saw them coming and grinned at the pair of them as they wobbled forward, Samuel in his classic blue and black snowsuit and Ana in her 'cool for the era' florescent pink and white Sunice ski coat. It was a coat she had begged her mother to purchase but now questioned, a coat that practically glowed like a florescent blinking warning beacon when she tumbled. "This ought to keep him entertained," thought the lifty.

"Break?" his co-worker asked, meandering up, granola bar in hand.

"No, not yet, I want to see this."

Every year they improved . . . and grew a few inches taller. Although, frankly, this wasn't as helpful as you may hope. The gap between them was growing fast. Samuel, younger by two years, already had several inches on his smaller ally. Last year they had developed a technique of leaning on one another on the lift. They found that if they leaned on each other, shoulder to shoulder, they could balance a few feet farther before a ski tip caught and one or the other was catapulted out into the trees.

Here they were, standing side by side with their bodies facing inward, awaiting the bar which they would grasp firmly. The goal was to grab the bar and rest it below their keisters before it lurched forward. Any mistakes at this point and the bar would launch them ahead into the preceding skiers, resulting in a faceplant and almost certainly some form or other of "yard sale."

Last year, the year they developed the shoulder-to-shoulder technique, someone's ski caught on a clump of ice and was twisted. After that the T-bar's crossbar seat got caught up in Ana's ski coat, raised, launched Samuel out of the way and hoisted Ana in the air so that her skies and legs folded under her perpendicular to the ground. There she was, momentarily suspended and dangling helplessly like a starfish suspended from a fisherman's hook as the bar then proceeded to drag its quarry a few inches from the ground and several feet forward. Toque, mitten and her left ski pulled from her body and tumbled in the snow before she managed to disentangle herself and roll out of the lift route. She sat up just in time to observe her stray ski floating, silent, graceful, and with ever-increasing speed downward towards the lifty.

Each time this happened, the retrieval took a few minutes, the pair hiking to the point of the lost items or shimmying down to the wayward item. Sometimes the lifty would stop the lift and allow them to retrieve their belongings, sometimes he wouldn't. If he didn't, then there they would be stranded like deer on a highway, dodging pairs of skiers while they darted downward again.

And then, after having wasted valuable time, tumbling, darting, shuffling back into position and waiting in line, they would be on the T-bar again, holding on for dear life and dreaming of the place other skiers were headed to, up, towards ski paradise, that place of powder and terrain that, until now, Samuel and Ana, had only hoped to gain.

And so it was, that, today, Samuel and Ana stood in position, took hold of the bar, and gave each other a nod as they steadied their skis. The T-bar lurched forward, launching them like an elastic band as they soared upward on the perfect foundation of packed snow. And this time, this time they held on and made it up the first eighth.

The little spruce marked the place where Samuel had taken a face plant the month earlier. And then, they were half way, beyond the place where Ana's ski usually stuck in a rut and tossed her sideways. They kept their skies steady and straight. A light breeze jostled the evergreen treetops, sending a cascade of glittering white flakes down on their coats and toques. They leaned on each other and kept their eyes on the track ahead. As the bar drew them upwards to the top third, they gasped with great big smiles of joy and glided higher, to places they had never had the skill to reach before, to the upper part of the hill above the tree line where only seasoned skiers and their parents had been previously and finally, finally, almost as if without any effort at all, they were there. Now all they had to do was glide out from under the T-bar and let it float upward to the pole as they gracefully slid into the landing area of skiers' paradise.

And that's when Samuel took a nose dive, and Ana panicked and let go of the t-bar which boomeranged around the pole, clanging noisily and barely missing a contact with the lift itself. They stared at each other a moment before recover-ing, sliding clear of the T-bar millimeters from on-coming traffic. There they were, at the top of the ski hill and looking eagerly with gratitude at the pano-rama. Kid vs T-bar. They had succeeded. They stood there a moment appreciating the glistening bowls of perfect white powder. Then they saw each other, all tousled by snow, and they laughed as kids of that age do, guttural and leg slapping laughter, almost bent over in giggles. They were going have one fabulous day.

Etnas

> *You will find as you look back upon your life that the moments when you have truly lived are the moments when you have done things in the spirit of love.*
> - Henry Drummond

As much as towns have wild pets, theirs has an ibex. She is lovely creature, more of a mascot than pet perhaps, graceful and loveable as any good ibex. Her summer grounds are the high pastures of the Alpen slopes. However, each winter, drawn by the groomed snow and open terrain of Rainville ski hill, where tufts of grass and shrubs are readily accessible, she makes her home on the hill, a handful of slopes and a few towers of its majestic splendor.

You can see that Rainville loves her ski hill and its resident. She has become a mascot of sorts. When a local couple opened the ski shop in the forties, they called it "Rentals of Etnas" in honour of Etnas the ibex. The hill is as much hers as it is the townspeople's. When Etnas grazes, ski patrol politely closes the lanes she grazes during the time of her sojourn, usually a few days per month, sometimes longer when she is drawn down to pas-ture by the snow and cold. Most years she brings her calves along to munch. Of course, like any mascot, Etnas is both timeless and (partly) mythologized. Sixty years after the naming of "Rentals of Etnas," the name of the local, seasonal ibex and her calves remains Etnas.

The kids generally respect this symbiotic relationship. They don't intend to trample into her territory one dark, chilly night of skiing, and it is only an unfortunate accident that the eldest two of them wear the official junior Seilbahnen Schweiz Ski Patrol jackets at the time. In fact, it is really just a fact finding tour, they claim. It is important to ensure all the runs, lit and unlit, are safe; however, at this moment, the so-called fact finding mission is really more related to ski conditions, such as, "Is there fresh powder on the east side routes?" Fortunately, no one notices as they drag themselves, snow soggy and weary from exertion and carrying their skis a half hour later. Well, no one notices "officially," though there is laughter shared in the retelling of it at the Parisian Café the next day.

It happened in February, when the weather had been so wonderfully spectacular that the kids had skied nearly daily, sometimes in the official ski patrol capacity but more often as regular skiers. Since there weren't many night trails to begin with, and half of those were closed due to the ranging habits of our dear Etnas, one can hardly feel astounded that the kids took a risk that night. The weather had become colder, and the kids could feel the twinge of frost on their cheeks and the wisp of cloud about their exhalations. They stood at the top of the closed run looking down into the unusually inky darkness.

Samuel had suggested this particular adventure, although the three eagerly lapped up the idea of adventure as they ducked under the yellow rope other patrollers had used to indicate the closed lane earlier in the day. The untracked snow glistened of diamonds as if to beckon them.

"We'll just check to see if anyone has gone down this route," they told each other by way of excuse.

From the upper section of the route, a soft glow from the lamps of a neighbouring course gently lights what the moon didn't. With or without light, the kids were expert skiers and knew the route.

Recently, the theme has been racing. The goal most days was to tuck from the top, lessening their wind resistance, in order to achieve maximum speed. During the day, they often set their stopwatches and raced each other from the top. One minute and a few seconds at the fastest, Samuel usually achieved that. A leisurely skier takes two or three times as long descending. They race this route so often that it has become second nature. Samuel has already broken one set of skis this year. One other ski was lost from the chair-lift at a neighboring ski hill. Samuel had been clapping his skis to the rhythm of an invented rap beat prior to the loss. This precipitated the adjustment of the binding settings to expert. As a result, the skis are set to highest possible setting. They'll only release under the direst of circumstances.

This particular route has an advantage. If one achieves maximum speed from the midpoint of the trail, a nat-ural dip allows the skier to gain "serious air." Gaining "serious air" means soaring from the top of the second hill to the bottom of the route without one's skis making contact with the ground. Tonight, in the silence of the closed run, the route appears deceptively empty as the trio descends. Samuel goes up ahead, gaining momentum and soaring as usual, right on target to achieve the perfect and enviable "serious air" and a smooth landing. The girls choose the more cautious route with S-turns and are just about to enter a tuck when the night air is punctuated by a sound.

Samuel, realizing that the landing pad is occupied by Etnas and her two calves, shouts in alarm. Both the calves and Etnas barely raise their heads from grazing.

Mid air, Samuel flails, realizing that he and the ibex are most certainly on a collision course. With last-minute calculations and contortions to divert disaster running through his mind, he manages to land left of the lumbering animal. His skis, as one would expect, tighten and do not release. Instead one snaps like a twig as he lands. Samuel, balancing and speeding recklessly on the one remaining good ski, manoeuvres, arching expertly, and sails helplessly around the ibex, narrowly missing the primary collision. The ibex, aware that she is no longer the sole occupant of this place, looks up nonchalantly as if to ask, "Who is entering my space?" and finds Samuel, stopped now, on his knees, in a kind of kinetic prayer position, precisely between Etnas and the two calves. Now, you know something about wild animal behaviour so I don't have to tell you how tense you should feel at this moment.

Mercifully, the element of surprise is on Samuel's side. It is in the moment before Etnas realises her situation that Samuel recognises it himself, the moment that Samuel, whose mind is quick to calculate risk, briefly anticipates and so before Etnas charges forward, he nimbly removes himself and slides to the side of the route.

Warned of the danger, the girls slow and though they can't quite see the danger ahead of them, manage to stop ahead of the ibex. Now this leaves a predicament. Half of Samuel's ski remains above them. That is easily remedied. The girls side step up the steep incline to reclaim the broken plank. It is then that they find that the only real route back to the main trail is now completely blocked by a startled ibex and her two calves. The entrance to the adjacent course and only other route back to the main route, lit run Ivrogne (Drunkard) is above them. Samuel is currently horizontally zipping on one ski towards the trees, somewhat gracefully to his credit. The other damaged plank he holds high in his hand. They have no choice but to hike. Looking down into what is now nearly pitch darkness at the shadowy bottom of the hill, they traverse towards the light of the main route into the trees and brush where they find Ivrogne, also unlit.

Fortunately, the entrance to Ivrogne is only a few meters beyond them. The trudge back is somewhat arduous. They find themselves hiking through knee-high, heavily compacted snow, fingers numbing and noses chilled. Along the way they retell the amusing anecdote of the true name of Ivrogne to each other to keep themselves entertained.

Today, the route is called something else but back then it was in fact officially titled "Chemin des Amoureux" (The path of lovers). This steep route is a charmingly narrow, tree-lined run. The name "Ivrogne" was a nickname given in honour of Markus, Ana's neighbour and ardent ski patroller who famously tumbled from top to bottom one night after a drunken pre-wedding ski with his buddies. Since his buddies were also members of the ski patrol, the nickname had stuck and the route was renamed, at least unofficially.

The laughter of recalling the dubious new title helped ease the chill of a humiliating hike, as did the warmth of hot cocoa and homemade cookies once they finally reached the safety of the lodge.

Within days, Samuels's skis had been replaced, and, as always, everything returned to normal. The three often took the same route again, after dark, via the closed route, on nights when the ibex was about in order to ensure the route was clear of stray skiers. However, they did so much more gingerly than they had before. There were many more adventures ahead of them all. Both Samuel and Ana were to miss turns and land in the midst of branches of trees, and one of their neighbours, Eric, would land himself so troublingly high in a tree that the fire department would be called, but these were in the future, and at the moment, all was well.

Summer Camp Adventures

Lac Antoine

Lac Antoine Summer Camp is a church camp, snuggled among the red-barked tamaracks in the majestic Alpine Mountains. This scenic place provides a spectacular backdrop to several camps each year, and a myriad of adventures. Families embrace such adventures whole heartedly. It's a Catholic camp; however, each summer when the weather grows warm enough to melt the ice at the tops of the upper peaks, the Lutheran community leases the Lac Antoine camp. This when the Andrewses have the most delightful months living in simple wooden cabins, capturing snapping turtles, frogs, and flags.

In the frosty mist of early mornings nestling around the cabins, there is serenity. Then, just after sunrise comes the piercing and melodic sound of a bugle as the pastor, a booming, robust man of significant fortitude, makes his daily walk from the pastors' cabin to the chapel bugling in the morning. It's a delightful sound . . . most of the time. This is how Ana and her family awaken every day, sometimes burrowing in and hiding beneath the blankets and sleeping bags until the last camp mates have risen to escape the chill and other times leaping out of bed to the cold wooden floors to start the day. After a prayer and breakfast, the day of adventures begins.

Turtle Races

"Live Well, Love Much, Laugh Often."
- Anonymous

CAPTURING AND RACING SNAPPING TURTLES. This is usually done in teams of two, though sometimes three. The best way to catch a turtle is to paddle one's canoe into turtle territory, usually close to the shore where the weeds and lake grasses provide good hiding places for minnows and bugs. Paddlers then must lift paddles so the canoe coasts into a meditative silence with as little movement as possible.

Turtles are relaxed and ponderously content creatures. They often swim just below the surface, reaching up with wrinkly green mouths to gurgle oxygen or nip at wet gnats and water runners that skim the surface. The apt turtle catcher observes their catch, places their hands on either side of the plate-like shell, just above the water and then smoothly swoops in, grasping either side of the turtle's soft underbelly and keeping one's fingers free of sharp claws or strong snapping jaw.

A successful turtle capture results in each team bringing

in one turtle. The teams return to camp and place their quarry into large batter buckets donated from the kitchen and partially filled with tepid lake water. The sight of one of these charming little creatures paddling about inevitably inspires others to embark on a turtle capturing expedition. As soon as enough campers have gathered their lumbering prizes, the game is to race the turtles back into the water as a way of releasing them back into the wild. The sandy, slightly downward slope of the swimming area leads towards the lake, making for the perfect race course. After so many years of this game, the turtles themselves are familiar with this summer routine and so have an inkling of what is afoot. They take the adventure with good spirit.

Teams prep their racers by marking numbers on their shells with a thick black Jiffy Marker. After several months of campers, marker tracing can be seen on each capture, indicating previous races. I'm quite certain there are several seasoned veteran racers among them.

It's Samuel who draws start and finish lines in the sand with a stick as Lione's buddy gathers campers by ringing the triangle.

There is an eager gathering with anticipation running high as the racers prepare to begin. Today, Samuel and his teammate Nina's turtle is turtle number 1.

Nina has done a practice run and her turtle appears in good shape, having headed directly towards the water as Lione, ankle deep in the water, manned the recapture.

Shouts and encouragement come from the gathering crowd as the turtles are placed at the start line and people vie for the best view, lining the beach, dock and fire pit areas. Friendly wagers are laid.

To the "bookie," Samuel's turtle is the frontrunner. This is primarily because has placed the only bet, a dollar. Ana and Nina grin and each add a quarter to the pot for a total of one-fifty from their team. Ana finds her place, and, on cue, gingerly sets down their team's turtle on the soft sand.

Someone finds a bugle, there are always bugles! At the call, the race begins. Turtles 2 and 4 make a beeline towards the shoreline in anticipation of returning home to the reeds and weeds of the lake. Turtle four lags behind, meandering as if basking in the delighted crowd as Turtle 5 makes a path towards the lush foliage of the councillor's cabin without pausing to hear his handler's shouts of direction. As the crowd cheers, turtle one has a good start running out from the start line before pausing. "The water, the water," Samuel, Ana and Nina encourage, while Lione beckons from the water.

The turtle has other plans. She cranes her wrinkly neck towards the water, then towards Samuel as if in acknowledgement before turning completely and heading in the direction of the refectory. By this point turtles 2 and 3 are a third of the way towards their goal. Turtle 1 is halfway towards hers.

"The other way!" they call.

Undaunted, Ana lifts her and returns her to the centre of the beach facing the water. Turtle 2 has stopped now and is observing the action. Turtle 4 is in fact almost there. At this point, turtle 1 spins completely around and begins digging in the sand, as if nesting for a few minutes, spins to face the water once more, then turns another 180 degrees and makes her way back up the hill. Kids and adults watch in amusement, cheering and laughing. There are again peals of laughter and dismay as Samuel's turtle, turtle 1, slowly and methodically makes her way to the pail and attempts to scale its smooth walls, thus returning to the shelter of her temporary holding space. Samuel reaches into his pocket and pulls out a dollar as the crowd erupts with applause. Turtle 4 has just crossed the finish line and entered the water.

Spy

Happiness is an inside job.
                                        - William Arthur Ward

To Ana, summer camp adventures usually involve making new friends; however, some years the Loockes join the festivities camping, and when they do, the dynamic is one of old friends and jubilance. There is the occasional trouble, a dark cloud on the perpetually blue sky. However, in balance, the summer adventures' scale is raised a notch on the years the Loockes join.

The kids don't always have a smooth go of things. The first week the Loockes joined the Andrewses at Lac Antoine, Samuel and Ana were practicing their fireman's chair, with both hands grasping the other's fore-arms to form a seat, when they accidently dropped Benjamin from a carefully constructed "throne," giving him a small goose egg and Samuel and Ana a scolding. Benjamin wasn't thrilled about this escapade. The accident was also spectacularly unfortunate given how carefully they had joined arms and hands into a safe grasp. Only moments prior to this they had agreed that they were ready to open business and allow "customers" to ride at the price of one dollar each.

The next week the Loockes joined camp, Trent's father raided their cabin after hearing the kids' shouts while playing "spy" from the top bunks. He burst in with that "caught you" look only the parents of creative and inventive children wear. It was a game-stopping look the kids knew only too well: they froze in mid sentence, mouths gaping. Some of the kids had water pistols. The kids were all crowded on the upper bunks in layers and bathing suits, with the exception of our "criminal," who coolly grinned from the floorboards while stuffing a water pistol under his shirt. Mr. Jamie banished his son and confiscated the water guns. After this incident, the kids were put out, moderately sullen and whining about Trent's father's sportsmanship. In fairness, I believe the phrase he heard as he walked by was, "Put your hands in the air, or we'll shoot."

As the day was a scorcher, the kids were sulking on the cabin stairs, whining about the loss of Trent and wondering what to do next. That's when it came to them that they pull a prank. *They* could follow in the tradition of summer camps, like the thousands of kids before them who had planned the most outrageous of pranks.

How the idea of pranking came to the kids is hardly relevant. Perhaps it was the popular camp films of the era, films like *Parent Trap*, where children are getting up to pleasant mischief. Or maybe it was because the night before some older girls from cabin four or five had come running into the fire area screaming.

It had played out something like this: The large group gathered around the fire immediately stopped their quiet chatter, half melted marshmallows hanging from sticks. They turned in the direction of the ruckus as the girls called with apparent fright:

"There's a bat in the cabin, there's a bat in the cabin."

The girls *looked* genuinely frightened in a way that caught and spread as though contagious. What a stir was created, as bats indeed did circle the camp site at night. Parents pointed towards the hills where they had often been seen after dark.

"Don't worry, bats usually live in caves and come out only at night."

"Yes, they do suck the blood of animals."

"Or is it only lick the wounds of injured cattle?"

"They don't actually bite do they?"

Ana looked up nervously from where she was sitting. She had hugged closer to her mother's side. She could see something circling high above the fire where moments ago they had been roasting marshmallows and singing camp songs under the starry sky. How had she not noticed it earlier? A few people expressed that they felt worried as bats may have been found in the camp itself, or bite a child. There was mention of rabies, and then a definition. Ana pulled gooey, toasted marshmallow from the stick and looked around the campfire for signs of frothing at the mouth. She'd heard about rabies. So far everyone looked safe enough. Dogs infected by rabies had to be put down. There was no telling what they'd do to a human found to be infected. After some discussion, two of the bravest of the adults were chosen. Armed with a flashlight and net, they went in the direction of the cabins to confront their collective fears.

After some investigation a baseball bat was found.

Now, the next morning, pranks become the ultimate game, one that if successful will earn the kids summer camp fame. The cleverness of the last prank has the kids stumped. How can they come up with something better than planting a bat in the cabin? They brainstorm one prank idea after another, and, sadly, come down with the most stubborn case of cumulative "prankster's block." No one can think of any pranks at all. Finally, someone comes up with the idea of soaking Mr. Loocke's pillow case.

"Not only his pillow case," Ana interjected. "When he finds out his pillow case is soaked, he'll swap it with yours. We have to soak all the pillow cases." It was the worst phrase ever to exit Ana's mouth and no sooner had she spoken had everyone stared agreeably.

"What will we sleep on?"

"We'll just sleep on our towels." Ana concluded, and somehow that atrocious idea makes sense. After some discussion, they come to a consensus they'll hide some of the pillow cases and soaking others, and that's what they did. Soon as anyone knew it all the pillow cases, of parents and kids alike, were soaking wet.

Of course by mid afternoon they'd been caught, most likely by a parent inquiring as to why their child was clandestinely drying their pillow case on the back stairs.

Within a half hour of that, a stream of pillow cases was hung up flaglike and drying in the sun. The parents took the prank badly. Still Trent free, the four spent the rest of the afternoon separated from camping friends in Hanna's cabin as a gentle segregation. Fortunately, the cabin was the cook's cabin and palatial, with nicely planed hardwood floors and large lakeside cabin windows facing out onto the lake. Then, a late summer storm broke. Since it was a rainy evening, they made up songs and played cards. None of them minded much, but now, a tone for the summer had been established.

The Garlic bread

> *Just as treasures are uncovered from the earth, so virtue appears from good deeds, and wisdom appears from a pure and peaceful mind. To walk safely through the maze of human life, one needs the light of wisdom and the guidance of virtue.*
> - Buddha

THE "REFECTOIRE," AS IT IS called, is a large, white, wooden barnlike structure lined with picnic style tables. The interior is decorated with brightly painted banners proclaiming inspirational camp messages and the names of previous years' themes and campers.

"Faith, Hope and Love," one encourages, "but the greatest of these is love."

"Love, Joy, Peace, Kindness, Goodness, Faithfulness, Gentleness, Self-Control," sings another.

Posters are vibrantly adorned with the acrylic handprints of previous campers, and names are signed onto the paper or canvas. These canvas and paper posters are strung around the structure on walls and above high, screened slat windows in celebration of fun, numerous virtues and life itself. These windows are painted white with clean bright paint. They are the type one can open inward to let in the breeze and allow one to hear the song of the birds nesting in the trellises outside, though, truly one could rarely hear anything above the din.

Outside, fastened to a tree behind the refectoire, a large, metallic triangle rings out an invitation to meals, prayers, games and gathering. For a clanger, it has a metal stick fastened to its top by a long rope, and while normally dormant, when it springs alive, so does everyone in camp.

Often, the ringing of the triangle involves several kids, all taking turns around the instrument. Whenever it is heard, it functions something like Pavlov's bell. Kids immediately sense hunger and are inspired to come running, salivating, perhaps drooling (although this hasn't been officially observed) and usually tumbling about one's peers and vying to achieve a seat next to a favourite companion.

The ringing of the bell is itself an honour. Once a group of children is selected, usually the nearest gaggle, or the team doing the kitchen preparation, the kids in it line up, play rock paper scissors to designate a ringer, and race to the task, which is usually done vigorously as peals of chiming emanate from the simple form.

The cheery "refectoire" is the hub of summer meal time and often the loudest camp space.

Hearty meals of simple classic fair keep the teams well fed. A warm atmosphere of clanging serving utensils and joyous voices nourish and give campers a space to catch up with friends and embrace the summertime activities.

Kids from a rural/healthy eating family savour some less healthy delights one wouldn't usually be served at home. These "delicacies," like Twinkies and Wagon Wheels, are high in kid flavour and fun. Foods mom usually reserves for school lunches on birthdays and, well, for serving at summer camp. One such brilliant treat is peach, tropical or grape drink otherwise known as punch. Grape drink is the kind of beverage they don't actually call juice since it comes from sugar crystals, ascorbic acid and flavouring. It's the kind of beverage that stains your lips purple or orange and tastes like nothing you can actually describe. "Well, you know, this has the flavor of grape drink," one would say about a sucker or gum of similar flavour.

With purple-stained lips and grape drink in hand, campers chat about fishing, turtle hunts, and water adventures or the results of the capture the flag game. This is a time that fishing stories grow exponentially, each kid stretching their tale with panache until the limits of their imagination are reached, the bubble is finally popped and the truth emerges.

"Yes, that rainbow-coloured flying fish that flew above the canoe, winked at us and then splashed back into the water on the other side."

"What?"

"Yes, it did have a snapping turtle on its back, how did you know?" The kids giggle.

"Okay, it was actually a large trout, and it did nibble on a skimmer bug before disappearing from view again."

More giggles.

Of course sometimes, a story is made more interesting when something unusual happens, a prank, a mishap, a funny moment, and this time, Ana's mom provided the fodder.

When it comes to the kitchen, Hanna's enthusiasm is rare and unparalleled. She whips up traditional camp foods like a pro. Recipes come from a well weathered "summer camp cookbook." This cookbook is a well-worn, often photocopied ring binder assembled by a committee of Lutheran ministers' wives and congregation moms. Its classic recipes include: pasta dishes, beans, green or pasta salads, breads, scalloped potatoes and so on, all perfectly spiced, cooked and served at just the right temperature.

Of these, spaghetti is a fan favourite. Of course, the long, stringy nature of spaghetti gives way to all kinds of creativity, and these are tested out on "silly spaghetti nights."

This is how "silly spaghetti night" night works: A large selection of cooking utensils are laid out on cooking sheets at the front of the hall: a potato masher, a giant slotted spoon, tongs, salad forks and spoons or perhaps a spatula. The goal is obvious: eat as much spaghetti as one can to fill one's stomach without resorting to a knife and fork. These meals take considerably longer, cleanup time is pretty much twice what it normally would be, and the children of families in attendance are often sent to the bathing rooms to wash themselves afterwards as food finds itself virtually everywhere.

Sometimes on "spaghetti night" the group links elbows to illustrate the importance of cooperation and unselfishness. The group leader tells the story of the man who, upon visiting heaven and hell, found the situation the same at each: Neither group could feed themselves since their arms were linked at the elbows. The difference between them in the end was their approach: in Hell, everyone was fighting and hungry, whereas in Heaven each person fed his companion. To illustrate this point, thus enacting a life lesson of cooperation and humility, campers linked arms around a giant serving dish of pasta. Unable to feed themselves, campers fed each other with messy and hilarious results.

This week, however, Lac Antoine had the usual utensils, and yet somehow, even with a knife, fork and plate, the meal took on a life of its own. It wasn't that the meal was special. It was ordinary spaghetti. The garlic bread, however, was . . . spectacular.

From the first whiff of baking wafting out of the kitchen window, Ana noted the scent of freshly baked bread and garlic, a lot of garlic. It smelled, well, stronger than usual. It wasn't *obviously* stronger, the bread looked as delicious as it usually did: steaming baguettes, sliced lengthwise with the same appetizing crust, that fresh-from-the-oven smell. The scent, however, was, well, *stronger*.

"Exactly how much garlic did you put in here?" Samuel inquired politely, amongst the mouthfuls of spaghetti and bread. The question of amount was pretty much rhetorical as it was obvious that several times the amount of garlic had been added to the recipe. Hanna leaned casually on the kitchen counter, slyly grinning. Several empty spice bottles of garlic powder stood in silent witness on the counter behind her.

"What do you mean?" Her face showed little sign of emotion. Inside, however, she was in stitches.

"Did you add the garlic?" she asked her colleagues innocently. No fewer than two other colleagues nodded.

"Is it too much?"

By this point kids and adults alike were nudging each other and reaching into the bread bowl for second, third and fourth helpings, tears of laughter and pungency streaming down their faces.

"I have a cold," Hanna confessed coolly.

The Far Dock

> *Do the difficult things while they are easy and do the great things while they are small. A journey of a thousand miles must begin with a single step.*
>
> - Lao Tzu

LAC ANTOINE IS GLACIAL FED. So, basically, snow and ice from mountaintops become water, barely warm enough to remain liquid, which makes its way into a natural basin people call a lake. Ana loves the water; however, she isn't fond of this glacial-fed bit. In fact, Ana isn't fond of being in the cold period. On crisp, chill mornings at camp, she wakes up first, usually before the sound of the bugles are played, while the air is icy and silent save for a few early song birds and when even the crickets have better sense than to hum until later in the day. She burrows herself beneath the blankets and sleeping bag layers until the other kids cajole her, call her name and promise her dibs for the showers. She burrows her feet deep into the bottom of the sleeping bag until her new camp friends tug her up and onto the cold

wooden floor. Then she runs to the shower rooms and, mild-mannered though she usually is, jostles for position so as to become the first in. This is so as to warm and dress as quickly as possible. Ana loves the warmth so much that, at night, she carries a blanket to the campfire and snuggles under it with as many as can fit, often more than could fit in fact, the outside two agreeably holding half a blanket and snuggling closer. It's crowded, and this is okay with her; the warmer the better.

So when Ana's mom agreed to cook for an extra week one summer, Ana finds herself as the youngest kid at the camp during teen week. Needless to say, she isn't impressed that the student lifeguard makes it mandatory that all swimmers dive into the icy cold lake and do two laps of the near dock prior to earning the right to swim to the farthest dock.

This level of hesitance is uncharacteristic for Ana. Usually, she relishes a challenge. This time, however, Ana's face takes on the determined look of someone preparing for the unpleasant. It isn't that the swim is difficult, though it is somewhat challenging—Ana is a reasonably strong swimmer—it's just that the water is . . . well, cold. Since these lakes in the Alps are glacier fed, they *freeze* during the winters. They do warm up during August, to be sure, it's just that they only warm up moderately, and the rest of the description, the part that isn't covered by "moderately" is, well, cool. "Refreshing" the adults would say encouragingly to Ana, who stands at the edge of the main doc shivering as she stares at them blankly wondering if perhaps they are using the term incorrectly. "Oh, *refreshing*. Of course." Usually, swimming to the near dock and then sunning or splashing and playing games is fun enough. These would keep her warm enough and mostly out of the water until the return swim where she would immediately wrap herself in the warmth of an awaiting towel. At this year's camp, however, the bar is set slightly higher since this year, the far dock is the cool place to chill.

The older boys go first, without hesitation. They dive in, in dramatic fashion with all the bravado one would expect of their age, the cutest of them slapping Ana with his towel in a comraderly way as he goes. The girls follow suit with shouts of encouragement. Ana, younger by a few years, doesn't exactly want to hesitate, especially since they are so kind and inviting. She doesn't want to seem ungrateful, it is just that the water is so cold and a swim of this distance requires at least fifteen minutes of water exposure before the actual long swim to the farthest dock.

"What if I just swim directly there?" She appeals to a stony-eyed lifeguard.

"What if I bring a life preserver with me?" The teen lifeguard is resolute. No proof swim, no long dock swim. Ana hides her significant hesitance by pretending to watch everyone else do it first.

Finally, she can't put off the inevitable any longer. She takes a deep breath, prepares herself to overcome the shivers and dives in. The first lap goes okay. The chilly water engulfs her as she swims, it splashes on her face and chills her arms into goosebumps so she swims faster. The faster she swims, the less she feels the cold water and the more she can focus on her breath and swim posture. Arm, elbow, tilt, breath, arm, elbow, tilt, breath. She counts her breaths, notices a shiver and responds by . . . how else? She swims faster.

This would have been okay. This strategy of speeding up to avoid the chill could have worked. It could have worked if she had remembered one simple thing: to breathe a little more between arm, elbow, tilts.

However, she doesn't remember to breath, and of course by the time she's completed the first lap her lungs are letting her know that they don't mind the cold as much as they mind the forgetting to breathe part.

Ana isn't listening to her lungs complaining. The water is cold and the sooner she finishes the sooner she can do the real swim out to the dock. The sooner she finishes, the sooner she can prove herself to the freckled-faced lifeguard, and the sooner she can join the others. And, best of all, the sooner she can sun herself outside of the water in the warmth.

She swims all the harder, picturing herself sunning on the distant dock, imagining the achievement keeps her swimming the next two thirds of the way around the dock. By this time, her lungs, which have begun making light complaints begin to cause her to want to wheeze in earnest. The desire to wheeze now takes the majority of her energy so when she finally reaches the main dock she hardly notices anything whatsoever. The lifeguard is peering down at her as she climbs the ladder, looking for signs of fatigue, and Ana, who wants nothing better than to gulp in air like a deep sea diver after a free dive, can't flinch a muscle if she wants to pass the test. She can't flinch if she wants into the far dock group of swimmers. She pulls herself confidently up onto the main dock, smiling as brightly as she can, and looking as calm as possible.

The lifeguard makes a close inspection, carefully examining her for signs of fatigue.

"Was that tough?" she asks. Ana nods her head, making sure not to say a word lest her voice betray her lung's complaints, she then picks up her towel and quickly leaves the dock, swaggering slightly as if in celebration of completing a great task. Only after she is out of sight does she bend over and catch her breath, only then does she suck in air wheezing. Standing behind the refectoire, hands on her knees and head between her legs as she gulps in large quantities of air, she feels a wave of relief. She grins with the satisfaction of a task completed. The far dock is much closer now, the barriers behind her and the sun is shining brightly. She's earned her place with the others. When she recovers sufficiently from the swim, she returns, walking as usual down the long main dock. Feeling the wooden planks below her feet as she slaps her neighbour on the back of the knees with her towel, she lies down on the deck to soak in the warmth of the sun.

"Is there anything that could make this moment more perfect?" asks her companion lazily while staring out at the blue expanse.

Ana looked up, "water wings."

The sanctuary sound system

> "Three things cannot be long hidden: the sun, the moon, and the truth."
>
> -Buddha

WHEN THE SERENELY UNLIT SANCTUARY lit up with the light of bold spotlights, and when from the PA system above came a voice into the silence, "This is God, 1, 2, 3, on you," Ana knew someone hadn't maintained their secret hiding place.

She froze in place. It was worse when she looked up into the sound booth and realized she didn't recognise this teenage "god."

"Our parents aren't going to like this," she groaned to Lione, who was grinning and pointing at the sound booth.

"Up there. Let's hide up there again," he was saying.

It was another hour before their parents' meetings were done. That's when the game of hide and seek ended and everyone gathered in the contest game room, also known as the foyer. That was several minutes after "god" had been caught and captured. At the time, he was playing heavy metal on the church synthesiser, with not only the spot light, but also green and red strobe lights flashing from the stage to the pews and panning back along the length of the stage.

Someone from the adjacent meeting room came to investigate after several noise complaints and a mysterious absence of *any* children whatsoever. Silence from the complaints department, coupled with what sounded like a rock and roll club starting up next door.

Explaining the situation wasn't easy.

"Well, the closet door was ajar and it seemed like a good place to hide," offered Ana, who, always seemed to be elected to explain, and "that's when we found a secret staircase." The excitement in her voice didn't match the tone of the inquiry.

Samuel gave her a look, and Nina nudged her elbow and she calmed down.

"And. . ."

"We followed it upstairs to the . . . 'pod!!'" chimed in Benjamin . . . and . . . we didn't touch *many* of the buttons."

"Um . . ." Ana glanced up helplessly, "well, Samuel did test *some* of the levers, but he put them back . . . it wasn't us who put the strobe light on."

Samuel groaned audibly and wondered why they always had to ask Ana. *She* never tells it right. "It wasn't the lever, it was the slide."

"Yes, the deacon had warned them . . . probably after he saw a string of kids entering and exiting the closet with hushed whispers." Ana was explaining again.

Samuel took a turn explaining. "That's when we went to play grounders in the basement,"

"We promise we didn't tell anyone else!" and with

consolatory looks at one another and their parents, and nudging each other, "Did you?"

Church annual meetings didn't usually involve stairways hidden in closets and darkened upstairs rooms full of mysterious lights, levers and buttons. Usually, the annual meeting of church elders was a boring affair, consisting of deli sandwiches made of white bread and served with mustard and an assortment of sweet pickles, and purple grape drink. Hours of kids finding something to do outside. This year, the year of the teenage mix-master, was the year it was cold and rainy outside so the only activities were indoor games. The only year it was rainy and nothing had been organized.

After this year's incident, and after the Church's sound person spent an undetermined amount of time reprimanding the teenager and then resetting all the sound settings from "blasting rock band party" to "Praise and worship mode," a group of parents got together and the next year they planned activities to keep everyone strategically active during the meeting.

After that, they turned the annual meeting into a bible-themed trivia event for kids with bible drills, quizzes and memorization games. The first year came as a surprise. Ana joined the bible drill team by herself, embarrassing Hanna and delighting Jacob, who egged her on with cheering from three rows back, and made a pretty good showing. That year, Ana and Samuel prepared as a team, and the next year, Ana's team arrived prepared.

Swimming lessons

> *Ability will never catch up with the demand for it.*
>
> \- Confucius

LARGE SPHERES OF COLOURFUL GLASS lights the roof of the neighbouring village's swimming pool, where the Loockes and Ana have swimming lessons twice a week. They've done that as long as the aquatic centre has been open. They love that place, with its warm, blue-and-white-tiled interior. Parents love the lounge with the modern windows of the warm observation area complete with large tropical plants and plush easy chairs. Carpooling means that parents take turns driving twenty-five minutes to the aquatic centre. That's a big journey when you live in a small European village. Before the opening of the leisure centre, the kids and their parents drove an hour into another village where they swam in an outdoor pool. Chilly water, and the even colder air of spring and autumn are made memorable with visits to the ice cream parlour, where the swimmers ate flavourful bites of ice cream with chocolate candies or fruit, their lips purple-blue and teeth chattering as they smiled bravely.

The opening of the new leisure center came with gentle smiles of relief. Now, the kids could swim all year round in a well-heated pool, and eat ice-cream from the cheerful wooden-and cloth-covered booths of the family-owned ice cream parlour. The ice cream is tastier, and the owners friendly. Sandwiches, French fries or ice cream are a treat to look forward to after most swim days. Occasionally, during the summer, visits to the neighborhood parks replace shivering in the back seat of the car while the heat vents crank hot air to a chorus of, "Hotter mom, we're icicles."

Today, at this moment, Ana is staring upwards, doing the backstroke as she counts the spheres of glass lights on the aqua centre roof. The red sphere signals the last few meters of the lane so, upon reaching the red sphere one stops swimming, puts both hands and arms behind one's head and drifts towards the ledge for the final meter. Failing to do this can result in swimming full force, head first, into the pool edge, resulting in a nasty goose egg. The pain is a deterrent; however, losing time is the true push as pausing to rub a tender bump with one's free hand delays the swim. Today, hand flat, Ana feels the ledge, does a back flip under water and swims once again, doing the front stroke this time. She can hear her instructor counting. "Breath one, two, elbow, hand, stroke, breath, one, two . . ."

Ana, glancing at the lane beside where Samuel is swimming at his fastest and slightly ahead of her, picks up the pace in what has become a nearly unbeatable final length. Samuel is taller, and slightly faster. That doesn't deter her, however. Sometimes she can win. Sometimes, she can race beyond him at the last second and reach the hot tub first, sometimes . . .

It isn't that they are inherently competitive, exactly. Okay, they are. They love a good challenge, and from competition springs a world where mundane tasks are made fun with the addition of game. This enhances their daily enjoyment and makes the otherwise mundane life of the small-town kids full of adventure. So it is that you see racing becomes a thing with their families. They race for everything.

"Dibs on the window seat," or "shotgun," shouts Samuel, running towards the front passenger seat of the car.

"Last one to the door is a rotten egg," yells Ana as they run towards the leisure centre's front door, the winner sledding into the glass with arms raised as if it were a home run. "Fastest swimmer wins first dibs on the best soccer card." And so it is that swimming lessons progress admirably despite the fact that most of their laps are swum as quickly as they possibly can be. Their swim instructor discourages such competitiveness.

"Racing won't help improve your form Ana," or, "This isn't a splashing contest, kids. Kick with straight legs," she sighs to half deaf ears as the racers speed past. If she had said, "Improving your technique will improve your speed," half the class would have instantaneously been listening with rapt attention.

Their parents are wiser. After a lifetime of raising them, they've learned how to utilize Samuel and Ana's competitive natures towards achieving their goals.

"First person out of the change rooms after class wins a package of soccer cards," Ana's mom encourages with a smirk, looking at her wrist watch and calculating how long it will take to make dinner. She even raises the bar by promising to set her stop-watch from the moment they exit the hot tub. Sometimes the prize is a personal bag of cheerio mix: cheerios, chocolate chips, peanuts and raisins. Other times it's soccer cards, of which all families have a collection, or a bag of chips. Today, the prize is soccer cards. The kids barter and ploy on their way into the leisure center, securing the terms before swimming began.

"One each! The first person out wins the best traders!" Samuel's mom Mary is classically maternal and feminine. She endures this constant jostling with characteristic, gentle perseverance.

Every time the result is a prize. Ana's mom has "smug" down pat. It is kind of like how green beans are a tremendous treat. Dad (who, despite Hanna's enthusiasm for Brussels sprouts, dislikes eating them, and can be seen pushing them around his plate) would say, "Brussels sprouts are only allowed to be eaten from my plate by little girls if they have done their chores and finished their dinner first." Games like these become a "camp" thing, where those on the outside of the joke play along and those on the inside, blindly at first and then with semi- to full awareness, achieve behavioural goals and earn the amusement and relief of both player and played.

Today is race day. Every day is race day. Ana's favourite part of swimming lessons is the ten-minute hot tub at the end of the lesson. She reaches the wall at the end of the last lap, jumps out of the pool and runs towards the tub, slightly behind Samuel, settling in beside her fellow swimmers who are already billowing their shorts with the water jets amidst peals of laughter.

She prepares for the next round. After swimming, the race is on once more. The girls, Ana, Nina and sometimes Katrina and her older sister walk from the deck (while in sight, as per the deal struck with the lifeguard) then race towards the change room, shower as quickly as possible, certainly not ensuring the chlorine has been washed from their hair effectively, dress in unison, and then, helping each other with buttons and clasps, run out the door as a group, breathless, giggling, and arriving at Ana's mother first and together, smelling of chlorine and soap residue, to collect their prize. Success!

The boys, it would seem, though they win most everything else, lose at the change room game. The girls have developed unique tricks to save time after months of contesting, such as leaving their lockers unlocked and brushing their hair after the race. Brushing their hair in the back of the car on the way to the burger place, or rewashing one's swimsuit in the sink at home, is a small price to pay when you have soccer cards in hand.

The boys never did figure this out. At least, if they did, it wasn't until they were much beyond racing, for with time the competition gave way to a more relaxed pace as the girls began to dry their hair, curl it with hot irons and primp.

At the moment, though, the girls are holding their soccer cards high with giggles of triumph, yawing dramatically and stretching so as to pretend as though they had been waiting hours, rather than seconds. The boys are only moments behind them as they race to the exit. They see that the girls have arrived first and, without needing to communicate, visibly slow their pace. With grins of superiority on their faces, they suavely, one could almost say nonchalantly, mosey towards the lounge, towels over their shoulders and bags in hand, pretending that they hadn't been racing at all, pretending not to have a care in the least . . . At least until the next day.

Ibex and amethyst

> "*The reports of my death have been greatly exaggerated.*"
> \- Mark Twain

THE RIDE TO AND FROM swimming lessons takes twenty-five minutes each direction. This equates to twenty-five highly enjoyable minutes to visit, sleep, do mad libs or play other imaginative car games. Sometimes the journey is as much fun as the lessons and, except when they are sleeping, almost always as entertaining. Other times, usually when Mark is late for a meeting after swimming, the journey has Samuel's dad gripping the steering wheel with white knuckles as he speeds home at speeds that are barely safe.

Today is one of those "other times," when M1. Loocke's knuckles turn white from tension about halfway home, and more or less remain that way.

It begins innocently enough, it always begins innocently enough, with the showing of some amethyst crystals Ana grew from the grow your own crystal kit that her father had bought. "Add the chemicals to the water to the point of saturation to grow a seed crystal . . . string the seed crystal from a string attached to a pencil on the edge of the container of saturated liquid and wait," the instructions read. "Beware. These are non-edible!"

The crystal growth kit becomes the topic of discussion on the drive to the pool as Ana explains to a sceptical group how she has grown amethyst crystals.

"They are actually quartz crystals," she explained. "They are really easy to grow!"

Samuel is full of questions: "How long does it take?" "Are they real crystals?" "Can I see them?"

The "Space crystal growing kit" was the result of a recent visit to the city on a bi-yearly shopping trip and, as the box promised, when you added boiling water to create a saturated solution of chemicals, crystals really did form. Sure enough, within a few weeks, tiny purple seed crystals had formed from the slurry at the bottom of the Purex measuring cup that doubled as an experiment dish. The generous and tidy selection of small seed crystals Ana had placed in a plastic zip lock bag and now displayed proudly seemed exceptional. They had a deep purple colour and fabulous clarity.

"See look!" she said, handing them forward to Samuel for closer inspection. "They're perfect! The longer you leave them in solution the larger they grow."

Soon the topic changes to which materials crystals can grow from, various household products such as sugar or salt are suggested, and the topic of the amethyst crystals is left behind in the flow of conversation that follows.

In the air was the chilly crispness of autumn in which the kids can see their breath as they bundle into the aquatic centre, Samuel holds the door as the group files in, cheerily relishing the task of appointing prizes.

"Let's make those crystals the prize," someone suggests. Ana hesitates. She'd grown these and they weren't easy to come by. However, in the spirit of companionship and with a good deal of prodding, she is soon persuaded. And so it was that today, Samuel, Nina and Ana were racing for a prize they really wanted, a bag of amethyst crystals.

As usual Samuel, with his lanky form and speed, wins the laps portion of the contest easily. Unusually, Samuel also wins the time challenge from the pool to the change rooms to Mr. Loocke, and the zip lock bag with its prize, jewel-like crystals, is handed over in good spirit.

It was too cold to have ice cream that day, and as it was early autumn and there was homework to be done, Mr. Loocke elected to drive directly home. With chlorine stinging their eyes and feeling the heavy, relaxed state after an hour of strenuous exertion, the kids were silent for the first several minutes as they drove out of town. Hypnotically, they looked out the car windows as the green station wagon ferried them beyond the river, their faces glued to the windows as autumn trees, barren of leaves and glowing soft in the diminishing sun, flew by as if by magic. As they rounded the sleepy residential area on the edge of town and arrived at the last turn before the length of farmland and forests that led home to their village, someone's eye caught sight of a herd of ibex. The kids perked up and a game was born.

"Whoever counts the largest number of ibex wins the crystals," Samuel challenged. Nina, who had been eyeing the glittery prize in Samuel's hand, wordlessly began counting, pointing out the window with her finger and soon the whole car was full of shouts as everyone joined in.

"Four, five, six . . ." four voices chimed simultaneously. "Oh, there's one up on the hill!"

"Seven, eight, a herd of them!"

"Nine, ten . . ." Ana and Nina pointed towards the herd.

The car wasn't traveling as quickly now, as if intuitively, Mr. Loocke knew when to slow down.

"Eleven, twelve," and that's when things got out of hand. "Thirteen, fourteen, fifteen . . . twenty-four, twenty-five . . . twenty-nine!" shouted Samuel with enthusiasm.

"Twenty-nine!"

"Twenty-nine?" Three heads counted again, "One, two, three, four, five, three on the hill, four, in the meadow."

"Twelve."

"Fifteen."

"Thirteen and twelve," again. "Twelve," Nina looked at Ana and Ana looked at Nina.

Benjamin was too young to count accurately. He sat in his car seat shouting numbers and counting on chubby kid fingers, staring out the window in front of them.

"Von, two, fwee, eeeghteen."

Nina and Ana turned their attention to Samuel in the front seat. Samuel, who had mysteriously counted seventeen extra ibex. Samuel, who was handling the crystals like a true champ, grinning as they slipped through his fingers and clinked back into the bag. The car was well beyond the hill now, moving ever nearer home, the ibex out of sight.

"We only counted twelve," they contended. After complaining for a few minutes in a spirited debate, Samuel explained the secret with a mischievous twinkle in this eye.

"Well," Samuel informed them in a voice that was quite used to explaining the unexplainable. "There *are* twelve ibex here. *I* counted the ibex on the other side of the hill. You can't see those ones."

Some arguments aren't to be contended with. It was agreed that Samuel would keep his prize for one week and then return it so that Ana could use the seed crystals to form the larger crystals as the box directed, and then the girls would grow more crystals the next time the families visited the city. Everything was silent for a few more minutes. Ana snoozed and sleepily traced the image of ibex and sheep in the steam of the warmed car window as Nina and Benjamin played a game of X's and O's. The mood was quiet and peaceful again. After a few minutes of relative silence Samuel handed the ziplock bag back to Ana. She took it tentatively.

"What is this?"

"You can have them back. I don't like them."

Nina's eyes grew wide and she sat up straighter in her chair, taking in the scene with keen interest. Ana paused. "You don't like them?" she restated in disbelief, staring down at the shimmering mauve crystals in her hand. After all this effort, the response sounded somewhat unorthodox.

"What is it that you don't like about them?"

Samuel stated the issue flatly.

"The taste."

There wasn't even a pause to indicate all pandemonium had broken loose. There was just a heavy silence.

"Samuel? You aren't supposed to eat them," Ana pointed out, catching her breath. "They're made of chemicals. They're poisonous."

Some words capture parental attention faster than

others. In an instant Samuel's father's face had changed from a placid lull to an alert, slightly flushed balance of panic and anger. The car jolted as he slammed on the brakes and then sped up again, momentarily uncertain whether to stop and return towards the clinic for immediate treatment or return home to Samuel's nurse mother. A volley of questions followed.

"How many had he eaten?" "What where they made of?" "How big of a handful?" and "What chemicals!"

The ride was tense and charged with worry. If Mr. Loocke had ever broken the speed limit before, he was *exceeding* it now. The kids sat silently, somberly observing as the pedometer crept higher and higher and the station wagon sped towards home.

It was Ana's father who answered the second question, cradling the phone in one hand and the box kit in the other.

"Silicon dioxide and iron," he said, looking at the box as if somehow knowing the name of the substance made it all better. A call was placed to the non-emergency/poison control line.

The following week at church Ana dared to ask the results of Mrs. Loocke's diagnosis.

"What happened?" she whispered as they stood side by side during the service. Mr. Loocke strummed the guitar and the adults sang a refrain from a popular chorus from their worn choir books.

"Nothing much," grinned Samuel. "Mom gave me charcoal and force fed me the largest lasagna dinner I had ever eaten so that I would go to the bathroom, and then I went to bed."

"Your mom's lasagna was the remedy?" Her whispering voice half incredulous.

"How much did they make you eat? Did it work?"

"Yes. It was delicious." He leaned in to whisper the rest as he jiggled the bag of crystals Ana had clandestinely placed back in his hands. "Thanks."

Pennies on the tracks

Love is the beauty of the soul.
- Saint Augustine

"Where are they?" Nina traced a smudge in the dust with the tip of her sneaker.

"Didn't they say they'd return by the time we were done?"

All eyes were on Samuel, as if magically, he would know the answers. He didn't.

It was fifteen minutes after swimming lessons had ended. The kids were clean and drying in the parking lot of the leisure centre, waiting. Waiting because -

"I'll just visit with Mr __ for a few minutes. Wait for me in the parking lot if I'm not back." Hanna's final comment when she'd left them there at the aquatic center an hour and forty minutes ago, had become . . . Well, that's what they were deciding. What had become of their parents?

Fortunately, it was a delightfully scorching day, windless, with bright sunlight high above, leaving a film of sandy debris along the concrete parking markers. A few, wispy clouds floated by, almost as if mistakenly placed in an otherwise clear sky.

And as happens when delightful mishaps become treasures of discovery, the previous autumn, they learned the most delightful thing: the timing of the CFF train (chemins de fer federaux suisses). As the train whistled and the CFF rail train came steaming along the track behind the centre, there was a tangle of arms and cacophony of sound as four kids abandoned their bags and ran with all their worth hooting and raising one arm in the shape of an L and pumping the air in a universal signal all train conductors know as, "blow the horn!!"

Capturing the conductor's attention wasn't easy. They ran clear to the other side of the parking lot, which was now littered with momentarily forgotten day bags and swimming goggles, shouting all the while. There was a moment of magic when the conductor made eye contact with the gaggle and to their delight there came the crisp, clear sound of "Whooot, whooot" piercing the warm afternoon, wisps of noise echoing among the poplars and along the valley.

The discovery of the CFF daily train schedule near the leisure center enhanced the weekly routine and from that moment on parents weren't only forgiven for their tardiness, they were *encouraged* to take their time and perhaps even to visit "that lady up the hill" while waiting for their kids to complete their lessons.

The first day of this knowledge was also the day that they came up with their ultimate plan, to place pennies on the track and wait for the train to flatten them.

"I heard they become the size of a saucer." Ana held up her hands in the size of an impossibly large shape.

This sounded implausible and, yet, enticing.

Samuel searched his pockets to find a penny and the others followed suit. They came up with a dime, a nickel and a few quarters, which they laid out in front of themselves on the concrete divider. For a few moments, they stood staring at the shiny metal spheres.

"I heard they fly from the track and can slice your ankles all the way to the bone."

"Really?" They paused to take in the horror. "We'll have to place them and then run back here until the train arrives."

"Dad says placing pennies on the track can derail a train." They pictured a train derailment, mentally wondering if they'd be safe from tottering rail cars at this distance.

After a few moments of silence, Nina spoke the question on all of their minds.

"Can they really derail a train?" This sounded both exciting and frightening at the same time and so there was a unanimous decision . . .

And that is a story of what didn't happen.

Albin

Albin

Patience is the companion of wisdom.
                                       - Saint Augustine

THE DAY ALBIN, THE FAMILY mutt, was brought home was charming, like something out of an old, 1950s classic American movie. You know the kind, the grainy films where a lovable, grubby kid hangs about the doors of the local shop sleepily sckootching on his haunches and drifting. The kid was almost asleep until the little cluster of bells hung on the outer door alerted him. There was Albin, among a litter of yelping, eagerly pawing puppies conveniently placed to draw attention. The sign in front of the mutts read:

"Free Puppies."

The kid, instantly recognising a kindred dog lover, looked up at Jacob and with perfect timing said, "Hey mister would you like a puppy?"

Twenty minutes later, Jacob, Hanna, and Ana, found themselves back in the Renault, a back seat full of puppy food, bedding and, of course, the family's latest addition. They named him Albin. No one knew exactly why.

As a family dog, Albin was a well-natured and mischievous mutt, a mixture of German shepherd and, well, no one really knew what. The neighbours had a Collie, so well behaved, friendly and wagging his tail and nuzzling gently with his Collie snout. "Like Lassie."

Albin was, more energetic. When a family member or neighbour came to visit, it wasn't a polite nuzzle one would be greeted with. Albin would run full tilt from wherever he was, wagging his tail and barking a welcoming song as if he was the one-dog welcoming committee. He'd jump up on the visitor, paws to the chest and licking as much of as he could reach. They tried dog training. This is where he learned how to sit and eat dog biscuits like a pro. He was especially good at eating dog biscuits. The other lessons, well . . . it didn't matter: the family loved him. He'd been "their" dog since the first day.

At first they *tried* to house him indoors. Hanna brought him a rawhide and one of those dog beds from the general store, which she placed in the hallway near the back door. Albin, however, liked sleeping in a warmer and friendlier place, Ana's bed, and so he developed ingenious ways of getting into the bedroom each night and jumping up onto the bed, licking her with his big, wet, slobbery tongue and then padding down with a few circles before curling up in the crease of her knees or across her legs. It was a habit her parents discouraged, since Albin spent a good part of his day digging and exploring and even after a pre-dinner rinse, padded around on questionably hygienic paws. For the first few months, Albin *did* sleep on Ana's bed, but then he developed intestinal worms and after he was cured it was recommended that he become an outdoor dog. By that point, Ana, whose responsibility it was to tend to Albin, didn't argue much.

But before the worms, before the specially built dog house that kept their family's pet outdoors, Ana and Albin were bunkmates and Albin played the role of the most faithful of companions. Ana was of the age where childhood fears where handled gently and with good humour. At the moment, those included a dislike of enclosed spaces and the dark. She liked to feel connected to the world of adults, and to sleep with the door open so as to bask sweetly in the soft glow of lamps and quiet chatter from the living room as she drifted into sleep. To facilitate this, Jacob and Hanna brought out the baby gate, the same one they had used when she was a baby and which had been stored until now in the crawl space under the house.

"We haven't seen this thing in years," commented her mother, as she un-slid the aluminum and wood panels and locked them against the door frame. Albin wagged his tail and nuzzled around their legs, circling figures eights and looking both innocent and alert. One would never know if he were simply a pup or a pup planning something like a heist, or a jail break. Unsuspectingly, they patted him on the head, slid the baby gate box back where it belonged, and went on about their days. Sure enough, a baby gate did almost nothing to discourage him. He jumped it without so much as clink and was found curled up against Ana the next day. Raising the baby gate didn't work either, although the first time he tried it, he misjudged the height and found that his feet got tangled up, yelping as he crashed snout first into the floor. Ana soothed him as he wagged his tail and leapt up onto the bed, promising herself to keep the knowledge of his ability to herself. So it was a day or two before a new strategy was needed and the "box gate" was developed.

The box gate consisted of four to six boxes, placed in the doorway, two wide and two high in the front. This was wide enough to discourage a lengthy jump and tall enough to work. The process was rather complicated and worked something like sealing a sparrow weaver nest or a cocoon. Each night, after brushing teeth, nightly prayers, a particularly beautiful ritual of kneeling down as a family, the three of them on the woven rug, holding hands together to express gratitude and special requests of the divine, Ana would curl up in bed and the process of sealing her in began. The boxes were placed in the doorway, two wide and two high. Although the boxes did manage to keep out Albin, the process invoked, among the giggles, a real safety issue in case of fire and had almost no effect, other than to alert Jacob of the "intruder." Once the house was quite and the adults asleep, Albin once again leapt the babygate, crashing among the cardboard as he smuggled himself noisily through and around the boxes and curled up in his favourite place.

Since Albin was a furry, hearty animal and also rambunctious and noisy, the family finally agreed to keep him outdoors at night. And that's when Jacob built him an outdoor doghouse with insulation, an entrance and inner chamber. Jacob found a design and spent days trimming and fitting two by fours, stuffing insulation and nailing carpet. The back deck took on the look of a true construction site and when it was done, the doghouse was truly a beautiful sight. This kept Albin warm during all but the colder mountain days and nights during which he was invited in.

During the day, he had the run of the house and yard. If he wanted in, all he had to do was scratch at the back door or whine and, with a little yip, inevitably someone would hear him and invite him in.

Albin and Hanna's Backyard Garden

> *Let us be grateful to people who make us happy, they are the charming gardeners who make our souls blossom.*
>
> - Marcel Proust

THIS WAS THE YEAR HANNA planted her first backyard garden. Hanna, a city girl whose parents were an engineer and a professor, had cultivated an innate affinity to nature and was thrilled to find herself raising Ana in the cozy, small town bordered by trees and wilderness.

"This space will make a wonderful garden," she said one evening to Jacob, who was standing beside her. He held her hand on the back deck as they looked out into the semi-urban back yard while dinner cooked in the oven. They surveyed the space together and designed the perfect garden area nestled beside the house. Later, they marked out an area with string and twine, leaving space in the yard to have a running area for Albin, play area, a sandbox, a compost mound, and an already growing rhubarb patch. The front of the house already grew strawberries. Hanna remembered the first year she'd grown them. Her daughter had found the tiny wild berries the way a child finds a hidden treasure. Gathering the little fruits and popping them into her mouth was the adventure of the day. Before you knew it, the first batch of little red berries had disappeared.

"I saved you two," she proclaimed upon looking up from her "berry meditation in red" to a horrified mother. Ana was holding out her earthen-smudged hand, palm up, invitingly. The last two tiny fruits were perched on her palm.

This year would be different, Hanna thought to herself. This year she would plant extra so that no matter how many grazing adventurers happened, there would be a plentiful harvest.

With great enthusiasm, Hanna chose a plot in the back-yard. She carved out a rectangle segment of lawn and edged it with cedar chips. This haven gave way to cabbage, potatoes, peas, beans, lettuce, carrots and rhubarb. The first year of planting, Hanna carefully planned and chose seeds purchased from the general store. She watched as they sprouted, watering them diligently and pulling the weeds. Albin observed from the porch or grass, wagging his tail and energetically joining in the activities. To him it appeared as though the kind adults were planting him his very own series of chew toys complete with sticks and flags.

At first Albin's affinity to digging didn't cause a real problem, rather simply a task. The neighbours on either side both had dogs. One had a pit-bull mutt and the other a Collie. The Collie, gentle and well mannered, kept to herself. The right-side neighbours, Jessica's family dog, didn't. Of course, as luck would have it, it was the naughty mutt and Albin who became inseparable. When anyone else was in the yard, Albin would follow about eagerly joining in on any activities of the day: digging in the sandbox, sniffing about, playing fetch. The neighbour's dog would also busy himself with the daily activities.

However, when those were done or when one of the dogs grew weary of their current activity, they would find one another along the fence, face sideways and route along the base of the fence, barking out a happy song and eagerly sharing sticks or bones or whatever treasure the other had found. It was truly odd, in fact, and within a few minutes the digging would commence, dirt flying in all directions as four paws and two snouts eagerly pawed towards each other, often with a bone, stick or some other desired object between them. One day they broke under the fence and the sunflowers, which were growing magnificently, took the brunt of the play. Another time they struck in the Andrewses' yard and this time it was the gates that they both managed to circumvent. Both pairs of adults were forced to postpone dinner as they took to the neighbourhood calling out the names of their respective dogs. Bud and Albin would dig a space under the fence so regularly that returning the other's dog and mending the holes under the fence became a regular task. Eventually, Jessica's dad, the neighbour, thought of cement. This fortified the holes created by their digging and forced the canine pair to find alternative digging areas along the fence.

At first, this doggie mode of entertainment had no impact whatsoever on Hanna's garden, but that was before the earth was turned and the seeds carefully planted. That's when Hanna's attitude towards the digging changed. This was Hanna's first garden, her beautifully planned and well-designed pride and joy. Watching your garden grow is like watching a miracle unfold. Growing vegetables is delicate, and her spirit felt a softening as she washed the grit from her fingers. One could almost say that Hanna, with her tough exterior and kind soul, felt a sense of profound satisfaction and happiness at having nurtured such a lovely space.

What Albin saw instead was a soft mound of soil and a game.

Hanna built a trench and edged it with more cedar chips.

The next morning, they found the soft soil scattered in a small section of the garden he'd chosen as his. Hanna didn't applaud. She replanted and had Jacob built a brim of dirt a few inches high. It was more of a boundary and deterrent than anything. Albin didn't take note.

A few weeks later, a small fence appeared. It was made of doweling and plastic netting.

A few nights after that, Albin crept nearly to the neighbour's fence, took a run at the fence and leapt the little protective boundary.

The plastic netting was chewed to tatters and the replanted carrots lay upside down in the disturbed soil. Some of the orange plastic netting was wrapped up in Albin's fur and tail as he greeted Jacob for dinner, his tail wagging excitedly.

Albin stayed indoors the next day, licking between his toes, and wagging his tail happily at the mention of the words "treat," "dinner" and "walk." Before replanting the upset vegetables, Hanna went to the hardware store and ordered several meters of chicken wire and several two-by-fours. The all-out battle to protect her garden had begun. A sturdier fence was more successful, although . . . it wasn't high enough to stop a master jump-dog as Albin. The fence became a high jump course. With this literal raising of the bar, so too were Albin's abilities inching higher. And with each increase the family frustration and determination in the mutt vs vegetable garden competition grew as well. Hanna planted the two-by-fours into the ground to create a barrier Albin couldn't dig under. The chicken wire inched higher. It became a battle of wills, with Hanna in one corner building ever higher as the cabbage and lettuce began to form, and Albin in the other, happily, one could almost say gleefully, exploring alternatives that would allow him to reach those delightfully round playthings the lady of the house was growing.

The orange plastic netting reappeared, this time a few meters up, above the chicken wire.

The garden became a veritable fortified space. There were two layers of chicken wire, one above the other, leaning a little with a bent and torn gap in the middle where Albin had found his way above and below the layers. That was the day Albin found an almost perfect but not yet grown cabbage and played fetch with it for a good thirty minutes, tearing about within the confines of the garden before he was captured and reigned in. Hanna threw up her hands in near resignation.

Nearer the end of summer, the neighbours on the hill added to the gardening woes. They complained that the story-high fence of chicken wire and two-by-four posts was unsightly. This didn't improve morale. An official complaint

was sent to the city council without a whisper to Jacob or Hanna. While the councillors were friendly about it, this was sorely discouraging. After all, Jacob and Hanna were doing their best. Jacob tried to placate them with promises of tidying, which did little. I do believe some muttering was heard at the dinner table that night, muttering about "mangy mutts" and some talk about these neighbours with their own chicken-wire peacock enclosure of their noisy pet peacocks. The peacocks that waltzed beautifully around during the day all spring, and screamed so piercingly loud at night that it sounded as if a horrific crime had occurred, waking everyone from deep sleep, and terrifying kids and adults alike before they realized what it was. There was some mention that this complaint may have been retribution for the anonymous emergency call to the police the first week the peacocks were brought to their new home. It wasn't Jacob who made the call, he pointed out; however, these neighbours, less generous than most, were annoyed never-the-less and looking to find fault, and so the garden fence, unsightly as it most certainly was, took the brunt of their ire.

Determined to protect the garden until harvest, Jacob and Hanna requested a few months more, September at least. This was, after all, their first ever garden. Finally, in the autumn, they dismantled the project that year, garden, chicken wire, plastic netting, two-by-fours and all.

I'm happy to report that the Andrewses, despite the challenges, had fine cabbage that year, and lettuce, potatoes and carrots. Despite the trouble, the entire garden grew delightfully with enough produce to feed close friends and celebrate with a session of canning beans. Albin did learn eventually, and future gardens grew reasonably well without the need for such barricades, and only a few losses.

Later, thinking back on that summer, Ana could recall the tottering, one-story structure and laugh. The gardens in their now "uptown" home were more successful. Here, Hanna had garden tiers built as a series of retaining walls into the side of the hill accessible only via a staircase up the middle. Truly, that was a wonderful and highly adventurous first growing season, the first of many and the most entertaining.

Albin and the harmonica

Oh, love will make a dog howl in rhyme.
-Francis Beaumont

OF ALL HIS TRAITS, NOBLE and ignoble, it is Albin's affinity for music that makes most of the family laugh the hardest. For some reason, he is fascinated by the harmonica. Other instruments intrigue him as any other dog. The guitar draws no particular reaction. It is the harmonica that has the most unusual effect on him. The sound of it speaks directly to some tone that calls him hypnotically. It is as if the harmonica is the flute of the piper of Hamlin piping his magic and he, Albin the mutt, the hypnotized rat. Being a logical sort, as far as dogs go, when the music begins, he makes a direct line to Hanna's feet.

This ritual happens every time, no matter where he is in the house. If she plays, he comes running. Running, running, silently on eager padded paws, he arrives silently, without as much as a peep from the farthest reaches of the house, unless of course he's outside. If he's outside, he scratches at the door and whines and sings until he's let in, at

which point he runs to her feet with the necessary intensity of a storm chaser to a hurricane. Then, when he is situated, tail wagging, seated and composed, he begins to howl and bark in time with the music. He howls as though howling at the moon, full force and with energy.

Whether inside or out, this is his routine. If he's sniffing around the cupboards in the kitchen, he runs to her feet. If he's curled up on the mat beside Ana's bed, he leaps up and runs to sing along. All this is much to her family's amusement and Hanna's chagrin as Hanna would achieve no more than a few notes before this lusty procession of harmony begins. At first they thought he disliked the sound of the music, or that it hurt his ears, and he was complaining and lodging a rather vocal complaint.

At first, they would remove him, take him down the hall, or outside. However, they soon discovered that this was not the case. No matter where they take him, he whines and strains until free. At the moment he achieves freedom, tearing at full energy, claws scratching at the linoleum, almost tripping on his own legs in his hurry to return to Hanna's feet. And always, after situating himself again, with a howl of what can only be considered contentment, he joins in the sing-along.

Albin and the daily walk

> *Correction does much, but encouragement does more.*
> - Johann Wolfgang von Goethe

NO MATTER WHAT HE IS gnawing on, digging up or howling at, his daily walk is Albin's favourite activity of the day, the part, he looks forward to . . . Okay, Albin has the attention span of a mutt so, technically, he doesn't actually look forward to the walk around the neighbourhood each afternoon. He spends the majority of the day fully engrossed in the moment's accomplishments of sniffing under the fence, barking at the ever-present squirrels or sleeping peacefully on Hanna's feet.

I say *on* Hanna's feet because he rarely sits *at* them, or even a polite distance from them, preferring rather to lay on them as heavily as he possibly can—her personal foot warmer. So, where he is otherwise engaged for the majority of the day, being a dog, Albin loves his walks even if he doesn't specifically look forward to them . . . But Ana does look forward to this part of the day from the time the school bell rings and she arrives home from school and finishes her afternoon snack of apple and cheese. And after the apple and cheese, maybe she'll play for a little bit, creating adventures in the forest with friends, and maybe she'll go downtown with her parents to bring the mail home, then dinner. After that it is time to walk the dog, and by that point, *this* is her favourite part of the day.

For Ana's parents, Albin's daily walk started out as a family activity, in those days when obedience training meant applying simple phrases to an eagerly inattentive dog. This is Jacob's task, teaching, as he patiently wonders as to the number of biscuits or laps around the park he'll have to do before "fetch" and "heal" become ingrained. Albin, at least, has so far mastered an understanding of the phrase "good dog" if nothing else. When he hears that phrase, he runs straight back to Jacob and sits nicely for a moment and a half, spins several times and nuzzles Jacob's pocket for a cookie. Well, that was a good start. Jacob encourages him to sit and hands him a dog cookie.

By degrees, the task is delegated to Ana so she can "learn responsibility," possibly slightly before Albin is ready.

"I'll do it," she volunteers eagerly. Lots of tasks are delegated so that Ana can "learn responsibility." Apparently making one's bed in the morning and cleaning up after Albin are specifically good at building responsibility. And there never comes a point when Ana says, "Okay, I'll leave my bed unmade today," because "good habits last a lifetime, and to tidy one's bed only takes a minute." So, walking Albin is more of a pleasure than a chore. They don't even call it a chore. It is just "walk time," another phrase Albin has mastered, upon hearing this, both kid and dog arrive, one dog and one kid with the leash in tow and a pocket full of biscuits.

To Ana's parents, this is one of the most entertaining periods of the day, because, while most owners walk their dogs, Albin, slightly smaller and lighter than Ana, but far more energetic and driven, walks her. He just seems to have an awareness of his audience and delights in making a run of it, pulling at the leash from the moment the door opens as if he were a greyhound released into a dog race that he knows he can win this time, tail wagging frantically as he pants and strains earnestly.

"I'll just run behind him," Ana says, grinning as she leaves the house at a brisk walk, heels and body tilted backwards in a facade of cool control as Albin pulls her along. "I'll just let him set the pace."

Secretly, I think her parents intentionally postpone evening gardening or working on the car so as to begin at this point of the evening, ensuring front row seats for the spectacle. Dad waves from the front lawn, grinning. Around the spacious neighbourhood block she goes, Albin running ahead of her, straining at the leash while she calls out useless commands, like "slow," "heel" . . . and finally, cookie in hand, "good boy."

I'm pleased to say that, eventually, Albin will learn to "heel," "sit," and "stay." Eventually, he does learn how to walk nicely, and then, in those quite summer afternoons after he has finally learned to walk nicely, Jacob enjoys evenings in his study instead of in the yard, quietly confident that his daughter is learning responsibility and that his every lesson had been absorbed.

The Great Outdoors

Spa day

Look within. Within is the fountain of good
- Marcus Aurelius

CLAY: A FINE-GRAINED NATURAL ROCK *or soil material.*
Purified clay is often used in the beauty industry to detoxify and smooth the skin
Dirt: Unclean matter. Common types of dirt include: dust, filth, grime, soil. (Wikipedia).
Dirt often contains mites and microbes, and while some elephants like to roll in it to protect their skin from sunburn, contact with dirt is not generally recommended, especially not before washing your hands at mealtime.

Have you ever looked back on childhood later in life and wondered how a piece of wisdom that seems so obvious and common sensisical could have been missed?

Nina, Samuel and Ana certainly did after one fine summer day in the middle of August.

That was the summer Ted's mom, the town's hairdresser and city councillor invited Ana and her mother into her home salon for a trim. The salon room was an imported taste of Hollywood, with chrome swivel chairs, large mirrors, and long white counters littered with scores of glossy fashion magazines.

That is where Ana learned about "the spa." It was in one of those industry magazines with a picture of a woman in a green clay mask basking on a spa table with cucumbers on her eyes. There was magic in that moment. The woman with clay on her face looked so *sophisticated*. Ever since that day, Ana had been researching and formulating home spa treatments: Egg whites to tighten the skin and minimize pores, honey and oatmeal to exfoliate and soften. Did you know that cucumbers and tea bags could reduce the inflammation of puffy eyes? And of course, there was clay—full body clay treatments where rich ladies in exotic locations were covered head to toe in warm, luxurious, body-purifying clay and set to bake in the Valencia or Seville sun for twenty to forty minutes.

And so the stage was set.

It was Samuel who planned the afternoon excursion.

"Wanna go to the river shallows after lunch?"

They were in Sunday school, gluing macaroni beards, and sequins into paper plate masks of Moses and Miriam. Sara was teaching them the song of Miriam, the one Miriam had sung to commemorate the day God parted the Red Sea to allow safe journey of the Israelites fleeing Egypt. Ana was imagining the wheels of the Egyptian chariots spinning aimlessly in the mud, and the Israelites arriving safely on the other shore. She held up her sequined Miriam mask with a grin.

"Sure!" Cycling to the shallows was one of her favourite excursions.

The weather cooperated, inviting them out into a world of nature. In fact, the weather was perfect, about twenty-five degrees Celsius and clear as clear could be. In high altitude mountain villages, perfect weather is rare and worthy of celebration. When it isn't a Sunday, sunny days are when shopkeepers make excuses to close the shop early and fish. Working adults make sangria and invite their friends to backyard barbeques rather than weeding that pesky patch of garden, or mending the car.

On particularly lovely sunny days, everyone is in a good mood. It's like an impromptu festival. Perfect summer weather promotes a mentality that is almost like the festive "snow days." You know, those days in the middle of the winter when heaven opens and the schools don't. Perfect weather beckons kids outdoors with the pleasant allure of bicycling and exploration. The best part is that perfect summer weather almost always arrives during the months of July and August, when kids are free, and don't have to worry about anything other than chores and piano lessons.

And so it was that after consuming a Sunday spread of luncheon meat, cheeses and breads savoured hastily, if there is such a thing, and after helping to wash the dishes, Ana rolled her purple BMC bicycle from the garage, gave the kickstand a tap, and headed out to meet the crew on the Loocke lawn. With blue, cloudless skies above and hours of sunlight ahead of them, Ana, Samuel, Nina and Lione set out on the winding asphalt stretch, riding the dusty, dirt shoulders and staying alert to traffic, which was mercifully rare on Sundays. They were on their way to the river shallows, a meandering tributary situated where the river broadens and slows down to meet the main river a few kilometres from town.

They didn't race, but they did pedal hard, arriving in record time by taking a lesser-known route down a slender, barely worn dirt path they had never taken before. They arrived at a sandbar of pebbles and silt at the elbow of the river, just shy of the river shallows.

If I could only describe the beauty of the place, it is like something out of a film, or a picture book of Alpine mountains, a vignette of nature, completely surrounded by the tall Alpines, with a little meandering brook watering the poplar trees and grasses; the cool wind in the leaves, the gurgling of a happy river and the merry song of birds and dragonflies the only sounds. The kind of place one might find a spa.

There certainly was enough dirt. "Silt," Ana corrected with a grin. "It's like clay." Well, almost. That was her first mistake. The others weren't so convinced at first.

"You mean like dirt?" Nina grimaced at the dark, silty matter settling between the rocks.

"Seriously?"

"Fancy women use it on their skins at spas," Ana encouraged them. "It makes your skin soft."

Well. Clay does.

Samuel, Nina and Lione were soon persuaded with promises of soft, glowing skin and within fifteen minutes Nina and Samuel had this delightful spa material on their arms and chins. Ana, however, was enthusiastically covered, head to foot, in soft, silty dirt.

"Are you sure about this?" questioned Nina.

"You're just afraid," returned Ana, slathering a handful of dirt on her arm. "It's fine."

Not so much.

For any reader who isn't following along, please pause now to read the section at the top of this story containing the definitions of dirt and clay.

"Now we leave it on for twenty to forty minutes and let it bake in the sun." Lying back on the pebbly sandbar with hands cupped behind her head, Ana let the hot summer sun bake the dirt into her skin.

Their spa day went reasonably well. The sun baked the silt beautifully and within the prescribed time they ventured into the clean brook water to clean the dirt from their skin. The remainder of the day was spent foraging a path into the shallows proper while discussing little curiosities of nature.

It wasn't until after returning home, just in time for dinner, that the ugly and itchy rash appeared. A red bumpy irritation caused by mite bites. The rash, as had the silt, covered Ana from head to toe. As it turns out, mites also love silt, and live in it abundantly. As it turns out, silt isn't clay. It's dirt, and far from making your skin soft, dirt is a haven of biting critters.

All three kids had showered and dressed in clean clothing before their parents noticed. And it was fully fourteen hours or so until they had to explain to peers.

"So, you gave yourself a spa day?" asked Jen as they lay on their backs on Jen's front lawn gazing up at the clouds. Ana blushed. "Do you think we had the wrong kind of clay?"

The mites left their mark slightly longer then they would have liked, but eventually their skin recovered so that when the kids met up again at the weekly evening bible studies, they were no longer dismally covered or itchy. Ana took in the scene, looking at each person in the living room at bible study that evening.

"I think the secret is that clay is purified first," Ana whispered sheepishly, as if consoling them and encouraging them towards the next adventure simultaneously.

"Did you know camomile tea bags can relieve the itching?" That comment received a silent glare from Nina, who was snuggled beside her, the four of them on a couch that fit three. Ana took the hint and remained silent for an uncharacteristically long period while the conversation flowed around her.

As it was primarily Ana who had suffered, she was soon forgiven, although she remembered her lesson. One day, she thought, one day, she will travel to a spa in Seville and bake in the Spanish sun, while the appropriate type of clay detoxifies and smoothes-such a luxurious treatment.

Camping with Black Bears

> *I offer thanks to you living and eternal King for you have mercifully restored my soul within me. Your faithfulness is great.*
> – Hebrew awakening blessing

THE ANDREWSES, WHO WERE ON vacation in Colorado, USA, where they had relatives, awoke one day to the sound of a motor-like bear hum, the sound a small black bear makes when it's routing in garbage. "Sniff, snorfle, snort." The sound a black bear makes when it has discovered what the garbage man won't for another two hours: a stash of orange peels from ginger marmalade making day carefully discarded in the garbage bin and deposited at the side of the curb for pick up later that morning.

Nina's feet touched the cold hardwood floor hurriedly as she scrabbled to throw a dressing gown over her pajamas and rush to the front door. She joined her parents, Jacob and Hanna who were already awake and observing the scene. Together, the three of them watched the black bear from behind the glass door on the porch. He was less than a dozen feet from home at the end of the driveway, rummaging contentedly. That was Ana's introduction to the State's most famous guest, wild guest that is. Several animals made their appearances. There was a family of deer also. These grazed on lush mountain grasses and tulip bulbs and were often seen around the schools where the forest was thin enough to provide both protection and nourishment. Over the course of years, the deer became tame enough to nibble tidbits out of one's hand. The bears, however, remained more elusive.

In the small village of Pika, Colorado, these aren't as rare as you might think. The local schools close one day or more per year so as to accommodate a bear and her cubs. Those are great days for the children who spend them trouncing around the neighbourhood with companions. The dirt pit area also closes from time to time to facilitate bears or other wildlife grazing, usually during the summer, as happened a week at the peak of summer when a cougar and her cub were rumoured to be in the same area. Ana was certain that her cousin Jason had started the rumour as a prank, but it was never confirmed. It did close access to the sand piles and exploration pathways for days as a precaution, forcing the neighbourhood kids to use the playground almost exclusively.

It was so blisteringly hot that Ana got sunstroke that week, despite her mother's warning to drink plenty of liquids and the slathering on of sunscreen. She and her friends spent the entire weekend lying in the hot sun on the park grass alternately on their elbows to observe the journey of lady bugs and ants across their path, and flat on their backs, so they could stare up at the clouds for hours and hours, creating mini-dramas from the poufy kinetic formations.

They learned to distinguish the lake gull from sea gulls, and the hawk from the falcon. It was a glorious weekend of laughter and creativity, until she vomited after dinner and had to stay indoors another day or two until Hanna, who is familiar with the heat and humidity of more southerly European summers, was satisfied that she was significantly recovered.

Watching local wildlife is a great pleasure in Pika. Townspeople encouraged the grazing deer even while complaining about the nibbled-on tulips each spring. They swap old wives tales and take moderate steps to keep deer at bay during the early growing season by hanging little cheesecloth bags of hair trimmings around the yard or fabric softener sheets in the hedges. Never-the-less, despite these attempts to keep them out of gardens, the deer, these graceful and gentle creatures, are loved. The same gardeners produce hay for them when the winters prove to be particularly harsh. They spend hours in patio armchairs watching as the town's herd of five to nine deer meander from lawn to lawn, making comments on their health and the size of the herd, as one might on a neighbor's new baby or visiting relatives.

And when one isn't looking to find wildlife, one encounters it, then tells the story as if recounting a meeting with a celebrity. That's because, in Pika, wildlife *are* celebrities. Dinner tables around the town are graced and made more interesting with the regaling of stories about the animals in range.

Camping also makes headlines at dinner tables around town and so this story, of Jacob and his little brown bear snore, became an instant classic.

It started in June or July. That's when camping season

begins in earnest around Pika. Some families practically move to the campgrounds with their sail boats and dune buggies and other seasonal toys during this season. Most of Ana's neighbours do. Every weekend is filled with swimming, fishing, hiking, campfires and all. The Andrewses usually vacation near their home in Switzerland, at the Lac Antoine church camp during August. Sometimes they join other families camping at the lake, and usually they stay close to town, where they have access to warm showers and home-cooked meals the following day.

This year they were in Pika, Colorado. And this was the year Mrs. Andrews decided that she wanted to "rough it" in a tent.

This fine summer day they drove the dusty roads of Colorado in their little rented car for an overnight camp out in a meadow and grouping of stones a few miles north of town. It's the clearing of an old stone hut near an Alpine lake that most townspeople refer to as "the hermitage."

Everyone was in high spirits. Amusingly enough, or as luck would have it, Hanna teased Jacob about his snoring on the way down. He snores occasionally these days, a new habit, that sometimes causes him to wake himself up in the processes.

"What was that?" he'd ask, jolting awake suddenly from his classic brown leather recliner and looking around alertly. Albin also snores. They compete. Sometimes Albin wakes himself up also, with a bark and a snort.

Ana knows when to vanish, and she set out almost immediately as soon as the car was unloaded to explore the trails. The dense green forest teemed with life and the smells of pine, decomposing timber and moss. The ancient paths led to the place where the few timber remnants and a tiny stone hut lay in a small clearing. Ana set about gathering wildflowers with the Majestic Rocky Mountains in the background, imagining the rugged, prayerful life the inhabitants must have experienced. Meanwhile Hanna and Jacob set up the complicated little three-man scouting tent. It's from Jacob's backpacking days when he spent three years traveling solo, hitchhiking in the seventies and working in wine vineyards, radio stations, and ship docks to learn about the world, even travelling as far west as Montreal and New York state. Today, the tent is more functional than it is elegant. Setting it up takes two people and tremendous patience. Three's a crowd. This was a process Ana had long ago learned was complicated and better left to her parents. Returning after a safe amount of time, the three of them gathered dry wood from the forest floor and built a roaring fire with one match, Hanna's specialty. Then they prepared dinner and fashioned cooking sticks from the poplar branches, whittling them with Jacob's Swiss army knife for roasting marshmallows. They heated water in an old camping kettle. It was actually an ordinary camping trip for the most part. The sun set with appropriate splendour behind picturesque peaks, and the conversation was minimal, the tone meditative. They discussed safety issues. Should Albin sleep outside or in? Should they lock the car doors? And then they went to sleep.

It was some time in the middle of the night when the sound began. Hmmmmm. There it was, the motor-like hum . . . .hmmmmmkerfloofy hmmmmm. Jacob shook awake and instinctively put a hand on Albin's collar. There was a scuffle as Albin sprang awake at essentially the same moment and growled a low, menacing growl. Hand on Albin's collar, Jacob managed to keep the family dog in the tent . . . and now he couldn't tell where the noise had come from. Did he hear anything? Was that a bear? He recalled the conversation in the car. He didn't actually snore like that, did he?

He thought he had heard a snuffling, like a bear sniffing out the side of the tent, perhaps the padding of a large mammal about the campfire. Now, everything outside was more or less silent. And then of course, he wondered, had he heard anything at all? Was that Albin snoring? Albin looked up curiously. His head and one ear were cocked to the side. He was listening. Albin looked at Jacob as if questioning. Had they woken themselves up? Jacob briefly thought about going outside and being non-confrontational to his deepest being, he's been raised in Bern, an urban dweller, but also protective of his family. He did go outside and saw a clear coast. Since there wasn't much anyone could do, eventually, he fell asleep again, Albin at his side.

It was as the first light flooded the inside of the tent the next morning that Ana first woke. She sat up and listened as Jacob and Hanna quietly discussed last night's adventure from a spot a few feet outside the tent. Albin, who could usually be found down the river chasing scents, raced about, tearing inside and outside the tent, running around the campsite, tail wagging and snout to the ground. He remained nearer the campground than usual this morning and soon he even returned to the inside of the tent, eagerly licking Ana's face, a slobbery welcome to the day.

Hanna and Jacob made coffee and bacon on the freshly lit morning's fire. It was bright now as Ana and

Albin tumbled out of the tent. There wasn't much sign of disruption, some scuffing about the campfire. They wondered if it had happened at all, and then there it was, the proof, as clear as day: two distinctive paw prints of a small or mid-sized black bear in the dust that had settled on the windshield after the back road drive. Two bear prints, and a little scuff, as though a small black bear had rather nimbly climbed up on the hood of the car and peered in, in search of tasty treats.

That wasn't the last time the Andrewses camped out, but it did enhance the tone of Hanna's snoring ribbing, and may also have inspired the purchase of a small campervan upon their return to Rainville a month later.

The Bare Bear and the Hospital

> *It's not what happens to you, but how you react to it that matters.*
>
> - Epictetus

THE HOSPITAL WHERE SARA, ANA'S aunt, works is located at the edge of Pika. The well-equipped facility is surrounded by a band of chestnut trees, and rests along the edge of the main highway leading to the major cities, across from which is the hardware store where contractors and home builders buy their wares. Beyond run the railway tracks that bring materials to the more urban centres, making the hospital both remote and reasonably well connected. The structure is a simple L shape with a helicopter landing pad. The long end of the L consists of a long corridor edged by patient rooms. The short leg of the L is where the administration and reception takes place. The long leg opens out into a patio or garden of sorts. That's where longer-stay patients go to smoke or simply relax in the afternoon sunshine. There is a small patio, a few wooden chairs, and some potted trees. It's a pleasant area of French-style glass doors, locked at night and often open wide during the days so that a breeze can enter. They do occasionally have unwanted visitors, usually an intoxicated local, although so rarely that the hospital staff couldn't remember the last time and certainly wasn't prepared for a visit on day from a little black bear, which wandered in, padding on little paws down the newly bleached tiled floors. He must have been curious, drawn by the interesting sounds and smells of the hospital or cafeteria.

Sara's co-worker was the first to observe this "guest" on her rounds. She jumped backwards and retreated hastily, leaping over the reception desk, although with considerable grace and calm. To her co-workers, she looked something like a professional pole-vaulter. Crouched down behind the reception desk, she informed the team, who at this point were gathered around peering down at her with looks of mild concern. Their attention then turned down the hall to their, um, new arrival. One that could be tagged, entered into the system, and treated for parasites; however, not by them. The appropriate authorities would have to be called.

"Um, 911? Local. Is this the police, please?"

"Yes. Oh hi, Sara. This is Stan, the dispatcher. Could you describe the issue please?"

"Stan, we have a small problem of a peeping Tom bear. Could you please send a detachment right away?"

"Certainly, there is a team in the area. Consider them dispatched. I'll keep you on the line until they arrive. . ." a pause while Stan directs the police crew by shouting instructions towards the guys in the office.

"Perhaps send a tranquilizer gun."

"Huh? What measures have you taken to secure the premise and ensure the security of the nurses and patients?"

"Yes, well, we've left the back patio open so that he can leave whenever he likes, however our attempts to carrel him have proven unsuccessful. The patients are instructed to stay in their rooms until further notice."

"Okay, good job so far. Is he armed or aggressive?"

"What? No, he's quite calm-probably curious. . . Did you say 'armed'?"

Of course by that time the police team was already on their way. The whole miscommunication was cleared up amidst peals of laughter a few minutes later when the squad car arrived with a blanket and a loudspeaker system. You know, so as to negotiate with the bare naked man.

The slip and slide

> *Start by doing what's necessary; then do what's possible; and suddenly you are doing the impossible.*
>
> *– Francis of Assisi*

THE WEATHER WAS FINE AND the kids woke up early in anticipation. This had been planned with the enthusiastic anticipation that comes with every August: water fight season. The first day of water fight season had already begun. That was the day they discovered that that indoor water hose wasn't in limits, the day Ana spent twenty minutes mopping the floor while everyone else continued across the street with mini water guns. Heather and Amanda and much of the cul-de-sac played along. That was day one. Today was day three, Samuel's parents unwittingly hosting what was planned as epic.

The night before, the four of them, Ana, Samuel, Lione and Nina, strategized what they would need. The obvious gear: A stash of balloons, water pistols, a new super soaker on each team, the garden hose, and a bucket and string.

Actually, they didn't use the bucket and string. It hadn't been necessary. The bucket and string were theoretical implements of water games, and also they couldn't reach the branches and didn't have access to the ladder. This remained locked in the garage.

They made teams. Girls vs boys, two vs two, and they could both watch out to protect Benjamin, in case he got in the way as he joined in, tottering about and getting under foot with his eager toddlerness and adorableness.

The girls tried to segregate themselves by announcing that the girls' planning meeting was in the basement and then retreating there with the door closed. Their parents were studying Scofield together in the living room, leaving little place to go, so the boys snuck downstairs to listen at the door using plastic Tupperware cups intended to amplify the sound. Of course the stairs creaked alarmingly, and the duo was caught. The boys were invited to join the basement huddle by parents eager to keep tabs on both parties at once, to the audibly vocal complaints of the girls. Finally the boys did contribute significantly to the strategy meeting. A funny thing happens when both teams share a single strategy.

But let's return to today. Today, the day of the epic water fight. Nina and Ana entered blindly and were classically outdone. It was fun at first. The water fight had been going on for ages, probably hours was Ana's best estimation. The timelessness of summer transforms minutes into hours and vise versa. Days, weeks and months flow into a single fluid moment. Both teams were drenched and run out.

Ana looked up from the front lawn as Samuel and Lione launched a full-on water balloon assault.

"Hault, stop!" she squealed, reaching down toward the

little pile of water balloons she'd been filling and suddenly needing an escape. Whoever thought of girls vs boys in the first place? Soaked to the bone and unsure of the location of her towel, barely aware of the location of her partner, who was arranging a pile of water balloons just in the blind area around the bend of the house in anticipation of Samuel and Lione, Ana looked around. This idea didn't seem so fun anymore. It was time to change the pace, it was time for an escape, and that's when the idea hit her, just after a water balloon bounced from her forehead and crashed onto the cement sidewalk in front of her.

"Let's play slip and slide." She looked up at a grinning Samuel. Then she ran around the corner, the boys in pursuit.

The idea couldn't have been more timely. They piled inside and made their request from Sara, who replied with characteristic gentleness as she pulled out the old slip and slide from its tattered, wrinkly box under the stairs and brought it back up to Samuel with a smile. She fed them sandwiches. Then they removed the roll and instructions from their enclosure and set up the long length of plastic down the hill and adjusted the sprinkler.

"What if other kids in the neighbourhood want to play?" asked Ana, always the practical one. They were standing on the grass between the two homes the Loockes owned, one a rental, one their own. Samuel, the 'how do we make money from this venture?' type, perked up at the suggestion.

"I bet we could make quite a bit of dough on this."

"We could paint signs and advertise," suggested Ana. Ana, who had a keen marketer's mind, although she was also the "let everyone join free" type.

"Why don't we print signs on Sunday, and then post

them at the store? We can hold the slip and slide extravaganza next week."

The weather forecast factored in and finally it was decided that the day's price of admission would be set at one dollar, unless of course, the joining parties were to bring something invaluable to the group, like another slip and slide. The Shepps paid up in advance and Samuel made two bucks before the thing even got started.

It took precisely ten minutes for other neighbours, who were riding their bicycles by, to notice and ask to join.

"What will you pay us?" grinned Samuel, a natural wrangler.

After a moment of questioning looks they chimed in, in unison, "We'll bring another slip and slide!"

"Deal," said Samuel.

That only left a sprinkler, and as there was only one hose, Ana volunteered.

She slung the heavy rubber tubing around her shoulders and rested it on the handlebars of her bicycle awkwardly, causing a wobble in the wheel as she struggled down the hill between the houses. Samuel's house was situated on a hill, the Andrews house on the other of two rises. Between them, two inclines, one up and one down. There was a hollow, flat dip between them and that is where the Byrnes lived. It was a cumbersome journey down her hill and back up theirs with a fifty-foot garden hose dripping tepid water from its bends.

Michael looked up from the dirt pile he was examining for insects as Ana beckoned him over to assist. He called to Katrina who noticed Ana and Michael from the kitchen window. She offered use of their skateboard and asked if she could join.

It took fifteen minutes for Katrina and Michael to change into swim wear. As it happened, they also had a slip and slide. That made three.

"Price of admission," stated Samuel, taking and expertly unrolling the slip and slid and grinning again, as they arrived to the Loockes' front lawn, skateboard, bike, hose, slip and slide and two extra companions in tow.

They set up the course reasonably quickly. If they had made posters that year, the poster would have boasted "fifty-four feet of plastic runway. Best waterslide in town."

The hill in their yard was a moderately steep little slope from the curb leading to a nice, long, smooth area. They set up the track of plastic as near the curb as possible.

The Loockes' house faced a road, and then a steep hill. The kids had to cross the road and climb the hill to take a run at the slip-and-slide. This was the runway. Since the lawn and grass hill part of the yard edged up to the roadway, the approach track, or runway course, went from the top of the hill, where a little bit of forest began, down an extremely steep embankment, across the paved road up the curb. Just on the other side of the curb you would dive onto the slip and slide!

The runway bank on the other side of the road was so steep that running at full speed created the risk of tumbling head over feet downwards so each you had to jog down the hill until touching the pavement with a toe, at which point you had to run full tilt across the street and hop the curb before throwing your weight down the slippery runway.

Sentinels were placed on either side of the "runway" in case a car came along. The sentinels would stand in the roadway and yell "clear" if there weren't any cars. At this point the chosen runner would run.

Two sprinklers weren't quite enough. Michael tried first, but he ran out of water three quarters of the way down, skidding to a stop, just short of the pool with an audible squweeeeeeek, followed by cheers and giggles. Michael and Katrina's mom Mia contributed a garden hose. Soon enough, the game was on with a line-up along each side of the course.

Hours passed as kid after kid climbed to the top of the hill, ran the route, and flopped onto the slip and slide in anticipation, each one slightly missing the mark. No one was making it all the way down the hill, along the flat, and into the wading pool. No one, that is, with the exception of Samuel. He managed it twice.

As the day sky softened into sundown, Samuel held onto the record. Samuel, the only person brave enough to run full tilt down the impossibly steep hill and the only one talented enough to keep his balance. He ran and slid the entire route to a cheering audience of kids and siblings. As he splashed into the water at the end of the run, Samuel became the hero of the day.

Epilogue

THANKSGIVING BROUGHT THE ANDREWSES AND Loockes together in celebration. Hanna cooked more than you could possibly imagine: homemade, simple and delicious. Mary brought her famous sour cream mashed potatoes.

And as they held hands around the brimming and festive kitchen table, they sang with gratitude the song they would sing to one another, and also to their children as adults.

Lord make me an instrument of your peace:
Where there is hatred let me sow love;
Where there is injury, pardon
Where there is doubt, faith;
Where there is despair, hope;
Where there is darkness, light;
Where there is sadness, joy.

O divine Master, grant
That I may never seek
To be consoled as to console,
To be understood as to understand

To be loved as to love with all my soul

For it is in giving that we receive
It is in pardoning that we are pardoned,
And it is in dying that we are born
To eternal life.
Amen

-The prayer of Saint Francis

Made in the USA
Middletown, DE
18 November 2017